★ 全民英檢初／中級適用
★ 學科能力測驗／指定科目考試／統一入學測驗適用

# 英文讀寫萬試通

政治大學外文中心副教授
車蓓群　審定
三民英語編輯小組　彙編

三民書局

ⓒ 英文讀寫萬試通

| 彙　　編 | 三民英語編輯小組 |
|---|---|
| 審　　定 | 車蓓群 |
| 企劃編輯 | 陳逸如 |
| 責任編輯 | 林佑禎 |
| 美術設計 | 郭雅萍 |
| 插畫設計 | 李吳宏　林靜暘 |

| 發 行 人 | 劉振強 |
|---|---|
| 著作財產權人 | 三民書局股份有限公司 |
| 發 行 所 | 三民書局股份有限公司 |
| | 地址　臺北市復興北路386號 |
| | 電話　(02)25006600 |
| | 郵撥帳號　0009998-5 |
| 門 市 部 | (復北店) 臺北市復興北路386號 |
| | (重南店) 臺北市重慶南路一段61號 |

| 出版日期 | 初版一刷　2017年4月 |
|---|---|
| 編　　號 | S 803360 |

行政院新聞局登記證局版臺業字第〇二〇〇號

有著作權‧不准侵害

4710660289306

http://www.sanmin.com.tw　三民網路書店
※本書如有缺頁、破損或裝訂錯誤，請寄回本公司更換。

# 序

知識，就是希望；閱讀，就是力量。

在這個資訊爆炸的時代，應該如何選擇真正有用的資訊來吸收？
在考場如戰場的競爭壓力之下，應該如何儲備實力，漂亮地面對挑戰？
身為地球村的一份子，應該如何增進英語實力，與世界接軌？

學習英文的目的，就是要讓自己在這個資訊爆炸的時代之中，突破語言的藩籬，站在吸收新知的制高點之上，以閱讀獲得力量，以知識創造希望！

針對在英文閱讀中可能面對的挑戰，我們費心規劃 Reading Power 系列叢書，希望在學習英語的路上助您一臂之力，讓您輕鬆閱讀、快樂學習。

本系列叢書分為三個等級：
Level 1：適用於大考中心公佈之詞彙分級表中第一、二級（前兩千個單字）的範圍；適用於全民英檢初級。
Level 2：適用於大考中心公佈之詞彙分級表中第三、四級（第兩千到四千個單字）的範圍；適用於全民英檢中級。
Level 3：適用於大考中心公佈之詞彙分級表中第五、六級（第四千到七千個單字）的範圍；適用於全民英檢中高級。
我們希望以這樣的分級方式，讓讀者能針對自己的需求及程度選擇適合的書籍。

誠摯希望在學習英語的路上，這套 Reading Power 系列叢書將伴隨您找到閱讀的力量，發揮知識的光芒！

# 給讀者的話

本書為 Reading Power 系列書籍，目的在於增進讀者的閱讀技巧，並進一步培養其批判性讀寫的素養與思考能力。本書兼顧理論與實務，理論方面涵蓋六大閱讀技巧教學。實務方面除了實際演練此六大閱讀技巧外，也包含寫作及批判思考能力的訓練，適合中等程度讀者使用，亦為準備全民英檢初中級、大學學測、指考、統一入學測驗等各項考試的最佳用書。

本書共分兩大部分。第一部分為閱讀技巧教學，共三個單元，涵蓋六項由低層次至高層次的閱讀技巧教學和演練：「文章大意」 及 「作者口吻和態度」(單元1)→「文章細節」及「上下文字義」(單元2)→「指涉」及「推論和預測」(單元3)。透過循序漸進的教學安排，讓讀者能先了解各單元所介紹的「閱讀技巧」後，參考下面列出的「常見題目類型」，再透過「小試身手」範例 1 及範例 2 兩個練習，了解如何辨識考題測驗重點，並應用這兩個閱讀技巧找出正確答案。「實戰演練」部分則提供一篇文章，讓讀者能正確辨識題目測驗重點後，更熟練地使用各單元所介紹的兩個閱讀技巧解題，提升閱讀能力。最後，讀者須以閱讀的文章為基礎回答相關問題，藉此精進寫作及批判思考能力。本書之第二部分則以閱讀技巧的實際演練為主軸，網羅十三篇不同主題的文章，搭配閱讀測驗題及寫作練習，讓讀者透過大量及反覆練習，提升閱讀能力與速度，並能以英文表達自己的想法與觀點。

本書附有試題之詳盡解析，方便讀者自修使用。本書之編寫，已經多次之整理與校對，若仍有疏漏之處，望先進不吝指正。

## 閱讀技巧篇

| Unit 1 | 閱讀技巧：Main idea、Writer's Tone and Attitude<br>Foie Gras: Delicacy or Cruelty 鵝肝醬：佳餚或殘暴 | 1 |

| Unit 2 | 閱讀技巧：Supporting details、Words in context<br>The Secrets of the Horror Film 恐怖片秘辛 | 7 |

| Unit 3 | 閱讀技巧：Reference、Inference and Prediction<br>A Minimum Wage 最低工資 | 14 |

## 實戰演練篇

| Unit 4 | Babies Are Natural Learners 嬰兒是天生學習者 | 22 |
| Unit 5 | The Rise of the Machines 機械的崛起 | 25 |
| Unit 6 | The Growing Influence of Webcasting 日漸壯大的網路直播 | 28 |
| Unit 7 | Tides and their Importance 潮汐與其重要性 | 30 |
| Unit 8 | The Ankh 生命之符 | 33 |
| Unit 9 | Otaku Culture 御宅文化 | 36 |
| Unit 10 | Color Theory 色彩理論 | 39 |
| Unit 11 | The Hippocratic Oath 希波克拉底誓詞 | 42 |
| Unit 12 | New British Law to Increase Safety of Women 英國新律法將加強婦女安全 | 45 |
| Unit 13 | In defense of Boredom 無聊萬歲 | 48 |
| Unit 14 | Beyond Our Imaginations 超乎我們的想像 | 51 |
| Unit 15 | A Belly Full of Plastic 塞滿塑膠廢棄物的海鳥胃 | 54 |
| Unit 16 | The Darwin Awards: Dying Has Never Been So Funny 達爾文獎：死亡從未如此荒謬 | 57 |
| Answer Key | | 60 |

# Unit 1

Unit 2 | Unit 3 | Unit 4 | Unit 5 | Unit 6 | Unit 7 | Unit 8 | Unit 9 | Unit 10 | Unit 11 | Unit 12 | Unit 13 | Unit 14 | Unit 15 | Unit 16

文章大意是作者依主題而發展出來的文章要點，也是作者想傳遞給讀者的重要訊息。透過略讀文章或各段落首句及利用上下文線索，都有助讀者掌握文章的重點訊息。另外，為了傳達這些訊息，作者通常會使用不同的寫作手法或用字來達成其寫作目的。這些寫作手法或用字的展現，就是作者的寫作口吻和態度。

**閱讀焦點** 文章大意 (main idea)、作者口吻和態度 (writer's tone and attitude)

**閱讀技巧**

① 利用略讀 (skimming)，找出主題句 (topic sentence)：主題句通常會放在第一句或接近段落開頭的位置，為簡潔的肯定句，是涵蓋全文或該段落的關鍵重點。可略讀文章首尾兩句，從中找出文章大意。

② 全文架構 (mapping)：若文章沒有明顯的主題句，可瀏覽每個段落的第一句，或圈選重複出現的字詞，利用上下文線索，推敲拼湊作者要傳達的重點，自行摘要出大意。

③ 審視作者寫作手法 (clarifying writer's tone and attitude)：不論作者寫作目的為說明、陳述、說服、傳達情感或宣導，從上下文的寫作手法及用字等線索，可推敲出作者的口吻與態度。例如，是否正反論述皆有，或只是偏頗某觀點。

**常見的題目類型**

| Main Idea | Writer's Tone and Attitude |
|---|---|
| · What is the main idea of this passage? | · What is the author's attitude toward _____? |
| · What is this article mainly about? | · What is the tone of this passage? |
| · What is the third paragraph mainly about? | · Which of the following best describes the author's attitude toward _____? |
| · What is the purpose of this passage? | · 選項中常見形容詞：negative, objective, admiring, suspicious, indifferent, optimistic, pessimistic, encouraging, defensive, neutral, etc. |
| · What is the best title for this passage? | |
| · What is the message that the author is trying to convey? | |

**小試身手**

範例一

Some people call it a traveling museum. Others refer to it as a living or open-air museum. Built in Brazil to celebrate the quincentennial of Columbus' first voyage to the New World, the Nina, a Columbus-era replica ship, provides visitors with an accurate visual of the size and sailing implements of Columbus' favorite ship from over

500 years ago.

I joined the crew of the Nina in Gulf Shores, Alabama, in February 2013. As part of a research project sponsored by my university, my goal was to document my days aboard the ship in a blog. I quickly realized that I gained the most valuable insights when I observed or gave tours to school-age children. The field-trip tour of the Nina is hands-on learning at its best. In this setting, students could touch the line, pass around a ballast stone, and move the extremely large tiller that steered the ships in Columbus' day. They soon came to understand the labor involved in sailing the ship back in his time. I was pleased to see the students become active participants in their learning process.

The Nina is not the only traveling museum that provides such field trips. A visit to Jamestown Settlement, for example, allows visitors to board three re-creations of the ships that brought the first settlers from England to Virginia in the early 1600s. Historical interpreters, dressed in period garb, give tours to the Susan Constant, Godspeed, and Discovery. These interpreters often portray a character that would have lived and worked during that time period. Students touring these ships are encouraged to interact with the interpreters in order to better understand the daily life in the past.

My experience on the Nina helps substantiate my long-held belief that students stay interested, ask better questions, and engage in higher-order thinking tasks when they are actively engaged in the learning process. The students who boarded the Nina came as passive learners. They left as bold explorers.

(105 年指考)

**此題判斷 main idea**

( D ) 1. What is the third paragraph mainly about?

　　　(A) Guidelines for visitors on the ships.

　　　(B) Life of the first settlers in Jamestown Settlement.

　　　(C) Duties of the interpreters in the British museums.

　　　(D) Introduction to some open-air museums similar to the Nina.

→ 答案為：(D)，因為略讀之後，找出第三段第一句 The Nina is not the only traveling museum that provides such field trips 即為主題句。而後面的 for example，便以詹姆斯敦鎮三艘複製的古船為例，說明這個露天博物館如何讓遊客體驗當時的生活型態，故可推知本段落主要介紹和 Nina 類似的露天博物館。

In Japan, a person's blood type is popularly believed to decide his/her temperament and personality. Type-A people are generally considered sensitive perfectionists and good team players, but over-anxious. Type Os are curious and generous but stubborn. Type ABs are artistic but mysterious and unpredictable, and type Bs are cheerful but eccentric, individualistic, and selfish. Though lacking scientific evidence, this belief is widely seen in books, magazines, and television shows.

The blood-type belief has been used in unusual ways. The women's softball team that won gold for Japan at the Beijing Olympics is reported to have used blood-type theories to customize training for each player. Some kindergartens have adopted teaching methods along blood group lines, and even major companies reportedly make decisions about assignments based on an employee's blood type. In 1990, Mitsubishi Electronics was reported to have announced the formation of a team composed entirely of AB workers, thanks to "their ability to make plans."

The belief even affects politics. One former prime minister considered it important enough to reveal in his official profile that he was a type A, while his opposition rival was type B. In 2011, a minister, Ryu Matsumoto, was forced to resign after only a week in office, when a bad-tempered encounter with local officials was televised. In his resignation speech, he blamed his failings on the fact that he was blood type B.

The blood-type craze, considered simply harmless fun by some Japanese, may manifest itself as prejudice and discrimination. In fact, this seems so common that the Japanese now have a term for it: bura-hara, meaning blood-type harassment. There are reports of discrimination leading to children being bullied, ending of happy relationships, and loss of job opportunities due to blood type.　　　　(105 年學測)

此題判斷 **writer's attitude**

( C ) 1. What is the speaker's attitude toward the blood-type belief in Japan?
　　(A) Negative.　(B) Defensive.　　(C) Objective.　　(D) Encouraging.

→ 答案為：(C)，因為作者整篇文章都以陳述「事實 (fact)」的方式，描寫日本人對不同血型的看法。文中未看見如：I think/believe/feel... 等表示個人主觀意見 (opinion) 的用字，或是其他作者表示讚揚、否字或批判的用字，由此可推知作者對日本血型信念抱持「客觀的」看法。

請閱讀文章，並根據文章之文意為當題選出最適當的一個選項。

Foie gras is a controversial delicacy made from the liver of a duck or goose. It is highly regarded for its rich flavor and creamy texture. The controversy surrounding foie gras is due to the method of its production which involves force-feeding and is considered by some to be cruel and inhumane.

The method of fattening birds has been known and used since ancient times. The first mention of foie gras is from Roman times and was made by feeding dried figs to geese to enlarge their livers. After the fall of the Roman Empire, foie gras disappeared from European cuisine until Jewish communities rediscovered that the fattened geese they used for cooking fat had enlarged livers with a rich and delicate flavor.

Foie gras was traditionally made from geese, but these days, duck liver accounts for 95% of foie gras production. To prepare for migration, some birds expand their throats to swallow whole fish for later digestion, naturally fattening and enlarging their livers. Ducks and geese are fattened by gradually increasing their feed over a period of 90 days after which they are forced-fed corn using a gavage for 12 to 15 days. A gavage is a funnel connected to a tube placed down the ducks' and geese's enlarged throats to enable force-feeding. The corn used is cooked with fat which fattens the liver creating its buttery texture. France is by far the largest producer and consumer of foie gras. It is considered a luxury and is generally eaten on special occasions.

The method of force-feeding ducks and geese with a gavage is believed by some to be cruel and inhumane with its production banned in many countries across Europe. These birds used for producing foie gras have been shown to be fearful of the person who feeds them and have heightened stress. While a duck or goose liver can naturally enlarge by up to 50%, the size of the liver in foie gras production increases by up to 10 times.

Debate regarding the treatment of ducks and geese for foie gras is ongoing. Ultimately, is it worth subjecting these animals to such an ordeal for what amounts to a luxury?

__B__ 1. What is the best title for this passage?

     (A) How to Make Foie Gras: Recipes and Tips

     (B) Foie Gras: Delicacy or Cruelty?

     (C) Force-feeding: An Inhumane Ordeal

     (D) Foie Gras: Classic French Cuisine?

此題判斷 **main idea**

_____ 2. What is the purpose of this passage?

     (A) To relate foie gras to the use of force feeding.

     (B) To prove the effectiveness of force feeding on geese.

     (C) To define foie gras and the method of force-feeding.

     (D) To point out the problem of foie gras and animal rights.

此題判斷 _____

_____ 3. What is the second paragraph mainly about?

     (A) The historical development of foie gras.

     (B) Relations of natural fattening and migration.

     (C) The rise and fall of foie gras in Europe.

     (D) How Romans and Jews fattened birds.

此題判斷 _____

_____ 4. What is the author's attitude toward foie gras?

     (A) Optimistic.

     (B) Disapproving.

     (C) Pessimistic.

     (D) Devoted.

此題判斷 _____

閱讀完文章後，請針對下列問題用英文表達自己的想法與觀點。

1. What is your favorite foreign food? Why do you like it so much?

_____

_____

_____

_____

2. As a consumer, are you for or against the production and selling of foie gras? State your reasons.

_____

_____

_____

_____

## Word Bank

1. foie gras (n.) (法文) 肥鵝肝醬；肥鵝肝
2. controversial (adj.) 有爭議的
3. delicacy (n.) 佳餚
4. force-feeding (n.) 強迫灌食
5. inhumane (adj.) 不人道的
6. fig (n.) 無花果
7. account for (v.) 數量上佔…
8. digestion (n.) 消化
9. gavage (n.) 灌食漏斗
10. funnel (n.) 漏斗
11. subject sb/sth to sth 使遭遇
12. ordeal (n.) 折磨
13. amount to (v.) 變成

　　文章細節是作者為了支持文章大意或主題句，用舉例、提供各種證據、數據、定義、理由等資訊的方式，來詳述或佐證其論點，而掃讀則是能夠幫助讀者正確找出這些對應細節的閱讀技巧。上下文字義題通常是作者在文章裡使用某個新字或片語來闡述他想表達的想法，這些新字的字義則可透過掃讀及尋找上下文線索(如舉例、定義、重述解釋等)，幫助讀者找到最合適的字義，理解文章內容。

**閱讀焦點** 文章細節 (supporting details)、上下文字義 (words in context)

**閱讀技巧**

① 閱讀技巧澄清：略讀 (skimming) 通常用於快速瀏覽每個段落的首尾兩句，以找出「文章大意」；掃讀 (scanning) 則用於快速掃瞄定位，以鎖定段落中特定且具體的關鍵訊息及細節，直攻重點。

② 利用掃讀 (scanning)，圈選關鍵字，並尋找文章中相對應的具體信息：作答細節型的題目前，要先看題目，然後將題目或選項中要詢問的「關鍵字」(如：時間、地點、人名、地名、專有名詞、統計數據、理由、舉例、原因、解釋、比較、定義、描述、隱喻等)，圈選出來。此外，細節問題的「題序」，通常會對應文章出現的「訊息順序」。利用掃讀找到關鍵字所對應的位置後，便可從前後的上下文中拼湊文意，找出答案。

③ 利用上下文線索 (context clues) 及掃讀 (scanning)，選擇同義字：作答字義題前，先用掃讀，找到字義題在文章中出現的位置後，利用此字彙附近的字詞，來猜測字義。這些線索可能是作者對此字彙所下的「定義」、「舉例」、或用不同的話來「重述解釋」，因此可作為答題的重要參考。

**常見的題目類型**

| Supporting Details | Words in Context |
| --- | --- |
| · **What** is the cause of _____ ? | · Which of the following is closest in meaning to "_____" in the first paragraph? |
| · **Why** is _____ difficult? | |
| · **Where** was _____ found? | · What does "_____" in the third paragraph most likely refer to? |
| · **How** is _____ formed? | |
| · According to the passage, **which** of the following statements is true about _____ ? | · According to the passage, what is "_____?" |
| | · What does the phrase "_____" in the first paragraph mean? |
| · **Which** of the following is one of the findings of the study? | |
| · **Which** of the following is NOT a potential benefit of _____ ? | · What does the author mean by "_____" in the fourth paragraph? |

範例一

Many marine animals, including penguins and marine iguanas, have evolved ways to get rid of excess salt by using special salt-expelling glands around their tongue. However, the sea snake's salt glands cannot handle the massive amounts of salt that would enter their bodies if they actually drank seawater. This poses a serious problem when it comes to getting enough water to drink. If seawater is not an option, how does this animal survive in the ocean?

An international team of researchers focused on a population of yellow-bellied sea snakes living near Costa Rica, where rain often does not fall for up to seven months out of the year. Because yellow-bellied sea snakes usually spend all of their time far from land, rain is the animals' only source of fresh water. When it rains, a thin layer of fresh water forms on top of the ocean, providing the snakes with a fleeting opportunity to lap up that precious resource. But during the dry season when there is no rain, snakes presumably have nothing to drink. Thus, the team became interested in testing whether sea snakes became dehydrated at sea.

The researchers collected more than 500 yellow-bellied sea snakes and weighed them. They found that during the dry season about half of the snakes accepted fresh water offered to them, while nearly none did during the wet season. A snake's likelihood to drink also correlated with its body condition, with more withered snakes being more likely to drink, and to drink more. Finally, as predicted, snakes captured during the dry season contained significantly less body water than those scooped up in the rainy season. Thus, it seems the snake is able to endure certain degrees of dehydration in between rains. Scientists believe that dehydration at sea may explain the declining populations of sea snakes in some parts of the world.　　　　(105 年學測)

( A ) 1. What is the purpose of the study described in this passage?

> 此題判斷 main idea

　　　(A) To test if sea snakes lose body water at sea.

　　　(B) To see whether sea snakes drink water offered to them.

　　　(C) To find out if sea snakes are greatly reduced in population.

　　　(D) To prove that sea snakes drink only water coming from rivers.

( A ) 2. Which of the following is one of the findings of the study?

(A) If a sea snake was dried and weak, it drank more fresh water.

(B) If captured in the wet season, sea snakes drank a lot of fresh water.

(C) Most of the sea snakes had lost a lot of body water when captured.

(D) Dehydration is not a problem among sea snakes since they live at sea.

→ 答案為：(A)，因為掃讀之後，將題目中 "one of the findings of the study" 圈出來，然後在文章第三段第 2 行找到相對應的 "found"，可知本題詢問海蛇研究發現的細節。 接著再用掃讀圈出選項(A)中的 "dried and weak" 及 "more fresh water"， 在第 4～5 行找到圈出的對應內容 "body condition"、 "more withered" 和 "more likely to drink"， 可見(A)就是正解。 圈出選項(B)的 "wet season" 及 "a lot of fresh water"， 對應第 3 行圈出的 "none" 和 "the wet season"，可知(B)錯誤。圈出選項(C)的 "a lot of" 及 "captured"，對應第 5～6 行圈出的 "captured" 和 "less body water"， 可知(C)錯誤。 圈出選項(D)的 "Dehydration" 及 "not"， 對應第 8～9 行的 "dehydration" 和 "the declining populations"，可知(D)錯誤。

( C ) 3. Which of the following is true about sea snakes?　

(A) Their salt glands can remove the salt in the seawater.

(B) They can drink seawater when it mixes with rainwater.

(C) The ocean is like a desert to them since they don't drink seawater.

(D) They usually live near the coastal area where there is more fresh water.

範例二

　　Ongoing conflicts across the Middle East have prevented more than 13 million children from attending school, according to a report published by UNICEF, the United Nations Children's Fund.

　　The report states that 40% of all children across the region are currently not receiving an education, which is a result of two consequences of violence: structural damage to schools and the displacement of populations, also called "forced migration." Both issues result from the tide of violence that has crossed the region in recent years. The report examines nine countries where a state of war has become the norm. Across these countries, violence has made 8,500 schools unusable. In certain cases, communities have relied on school buildings to function as shelters for the displaced, with up to nine families living in a single classroom in former schools across **Iraq**.

The report pays particularly close attention to Syria, where a bloody civil war has displaced at least nine million people since the war began in 2011. With the crisis now in its fifth year, basic public services, including education, inside Syria have been stretched to breaking point. Within the country, the quality and availability of education depends on whether a particular region is suffering violence.

The report concludes with an earnest request to international policymakers to distribute financial and other resources to ease the regional crisis. With more than 13 million children already driven from classrooms by conflict, it is no exaggeration to say that the educational prospects of a generation of children are **in the balance**. The forces that are crushing individual lives and futures are also destroying the prospects for an entire region.

(105 年學測)

此題判斷 main idea

( D ) 1. What is this article mainly about?
  (A) Why people are moving away from their own countries.
  (B) Why there are civil wars and violence in the Middle East.
  (C) Why many schools have become shelters for displaced families.
  (D) Why many children in the Middle East are not attending school.

此題判斷 words in context

( B ) 2. What does the phrase "**in the balance**" in the last paragraph most likely mean?
  (A) Being well taken care of.　　(B) In an uncertain situation.
  (C) Under control by the authority.　(D) Moving in the wrong direction.

→ 答案為：(B)，因為用掃讀後，在最後一段第 4 行找到對應的目標片語。接著利用上下文線索，掃讀圈出上一句的關鍵字 "children driven from classrooms"，及下一句的 "destroying the prospects"，可知此地區的衝突對兒童教育前景是負面影響，故可刪去(A)與(C)。最後，由第 2 行的 "the regional crisis" 可推知，此區兒童教育前景因衝突「處於危急、不確定的狀況」，並未提及任何兒童教育政策的方向，故選(B)，不選(D)。

( D ) 3. According to the passage, which of the following statements is true? 此題判斷 supporting details

(A) The war in Syria has been going on since 2011.

(B) More than nine thousand schools have been destroyed by wars.

(C) Thirteen million people have been forced to leave their homes in the Middle East.

(D) Forty percent of all children in the world are not attending schools due to ongoing conflict.

## ⏱ 實戰演練

請閱讀文章，並根據文章之文意為當題選出最適當的一個選項。

What makes you scared? Do you think that you could channel that fear into making a horror film? If you think it would be easy, then think again.

Making horror films is a very difficult thing to do. Filmmakers must have a deep understanding about what it is that truly scares people, and they must use the psychology of fear to make their films. A.D. Calvo writes in *Filmmaker Magazine* that there are many different aspects of a good horror film. While understanding what it is that scares you is always important, it must be presented using a proper atmosphere. He describes this as "a moody visual undertone" that brings out a general feeling of dread in the audience. In addition to this, there must be **suspense**. If you know what is going to happen next, why would you be surprised? Keeping the audience in the dark about exactly what is happening is a great way to generate screams.

Calvo also mentions different framing techniques, such as shooting through branches or from behind a curtain. When seen this way, it helps give the audience the perspective of the **sinister** force in the film. It helps the audience understand that someone or something is watching. These techniques also help set a creepy mood, as do lighting, sound effects, and even the film score.

One important part of many horror films is known as the jump scare. This is when something on screen happens that literally causes you to jump in your seat because you are suddenly frightened. Jump scares can be real, such as when a terrible monster suddenly appears, or they can be "false." A "false" jump scare is when something happens that is unrelated to the plot but still startles the audience. A sudden sound, such as a cat in the room knocking over a glass that smashes on the floor, can produce a false jump scare.

In the end, there is a lot involved in the making of horror films, and it's not an easy genre to master. However, if you use some tried and tested techniques, though, you might find success as a horror filmmaker.

_C_ 1. According to the passage, which of the following 此題判斷 **supporting details** was NOT mentioned as a necessary aspect of a good horror film?
(A) The psychology of fear.  (B) A creepy atmosphere.
(C) A supernatural creature.  (D) The use of suspense.

_____ 2. Which of the following description about framing 此題判斷 _____ techniques is true?
(A) Shooting a film before a curtain creates a fearsome atmosphere.
(B) Lighting, sound effects and the film score can cause dread in viewers.
(C) A real jump scare alone cannot cause extreme fear in audience.
(D) The appearance of a horrible monster can produce a false jump scare.

_____ 3. What does the word "**suspense**" in the second 此題判斷 _____ paragraph mean?
(A) Fear of feeling moody.  (B) Dread of death.
(C) Screams of horror.  (D) Delay of telling something.

_____ 4. Which of the following is closest in meaning to 此題判斷 _____ "**sinister**" in the third paragraph?
(A) Fair.  (B) Amazing.
(C) Evil.  (D) Mental.

閱讀完文章後，請針對下列問題用英文表達自己的想法與觀點。

1. Do you like horror movies? Why or why not?

_____

_____

_____

_____

2. Below are two film posters. Look at the film titles on the posters and guess what the two films will be about. Which one will you choose to watch? Why?

(Please state the reasons why you make such a choice first; then make a guess and briefly describe the storyline of the film you choose.)

The Incredible Journey

The Missing Girl

_____

_____

_____

_____

## Word Bank

1. channel (v.) 傳送

2. undertone (n.) 潛在含意

3. suspense (n.) 懸疑

4. keep sb in the dark 將某人蒙在鼓裡

5. sinister (adj.) 邪惡不祥的

6. score (n.) 配樂

7. jump scare (n.) 突如其來的驚嚇
   (恐怖片拍攝手法)

8. knock over (v.) 撞倒；打翻

9. genre (n.) 類型

指涉型題目是指作者為使文章內容更加連貫與清晰，會在文章裡使用代名詞或關係代名詞等，來代替重覆出現的名詞及概念，通常讀者只要利用上下文線索，便能推敲此指涉詞所代替的內容為何。推論和預測型問題通常需要讀者在了解文章內容後，利用文章裡作者暗示的訊息，結合自己的背景知識及邏輯批判思考能力，來導出結論並對事實作進一步解讀與預測。

**閱讀焦點** 指涉 (reference)、推論 (inference) 以及預測 (prediction)

**閱讀技巧**

①利用上下文線索 (context clues)，找出指涉的對象：在文章中，作者常會使用「代名詞」(如 it, this, that, they, one...)、「關係代名詞」(如 which, that...)、「一般名詞」(如 the project, the memory...)、或是「副詞」(如 so)，來代替「前面」已經出現過的單字、片語、或句子。因此利用「上下文線索」，便能正確在「前面」出現的名詞或句子中，推敲出這個代名詞所指涉的對象。找出可能的答案後，再放入指涉題出現的句子中看看是否合理。

②運用批判思考能力 (critical thinking)，推論文章隱含訊息，並預測接下來的發展：推論型的問題中，作者常會在文中透露暗示性的訊息，或是提供客觀事實與細節，讓讀者自己從這些隱藏或明示的訊息中，推論可能的答案。作答時，可先「略讀」文章後，拼湊「上下文線索」，並留意作者在段落之間所使用的「轉折字」，最後再運用批判思考能力，作出合邏輯的推論。針對預測型的問題，則須仔細觀察作者在「最後一段」所提供的線索及語意，運用批判思考能力，合理預測文章下一步的發展。

**常見的題目類型**

| Reference | Inference and Prediction |
|---|---|
| · Who does "**they/that/this/it**" in the third paragraph most likely refer to?<br>· What does the word "**so**" in the first paragraph refer to?<br>· What does "**the project**" in the second paragraph refer to?<br>· Which of the following is the most appropriate interpretation of "**its**" in the last paragraph? | · Which of the following can be inferred from the passage?<br>· According to the passage, what would ＿＿ most likely do?<br>· By whom was the passage most likely written?<br>· Who would most likely be interested in the information found in this passage?<br>· This passage would most likely be found in a magazine about ＿＿.<br>· What does the author mean by the last two sentences of the passage?<br>· What will the next paragraph discuss according to the last paragraph?<br>· As more similar cases are reported, what will happen next? |

Screaming is one of the primal responses humans share with other animals. Conventional thinking suggests that what sets a scream apart from other sounds is its loudness or high pitch. However, many sounds that are loud and high-pitched do not raise goose bumps like screams can. To find out what makes human screams unique, neuroscientist Luc Arnal and his team examined a bank of sounds containing sentences spoken or screamed by 19 adults. The result shows screams and screamed sentences had a quality called "roughness," which refers to how fast a sound changes in loudness. While normal speech sounds only have slight differences in loudness—between 4 and 5 Hz, screams can switch very fast, varying between 30 and 150 Hz, thus perceived as being rough and unpleasant.

Arnal's team asked 20 subjects to judge screams as neutral or fearful, and found that the scariest almost always corresponded with roughness. The team then studied how the human brain responds to roughness using fMRI brain scanners. As expected, after hearing a scream, activity increased in the brain's auditory centers where sound coming into the ears is processed. But the scans also lit up in the amygdala, the brain's fear center.

The amygdala is the area that regulates our emotional and physiological response to danger. When a threat is detected, our adrenaline rises, and our body prepares to react to danger. The study discovered that screams have a similar influence on our body. It also found that roughness isn't heard when we speak naturally, regardless of the language we use, but **it** is prevalent in artificial sounds. The most aggravating alarm clocks, car horns, and fire alarms possess high degrees of roughness.

One potential application for this research might be to add roughness to alarm sounds to make them more effective, the same way a bad smell is added to natural gas to make it easily detectable. Warning sounds could also be added to electric cars, which are particularly silent, so they can be efficiently detected by pedestrians. (105 年指考)

( C ) 1. What is the first paragraph mainly about?

此題判斷 main idea

    (A) Different types of screams.

    (B) Human sounds and animal cries.

    (C) Specific features of screams.

    (D) Sound changes and goose bumps.

( B ) 2. According to the passage, which of the following is NOT a finding by Arnal's team?

此題判斷 supporting details

    (A) Changes in volume make screams different from other sounds.

    (B) Only humans can produce sounds with great loudness variation.

    (C) Normal human speech sounds vary between 4 to 5 Hz in loudness.

    (D) Drastic volume variation in speech can effectively activate the amygdala.

此題判斷 reference

( C ) 3. What does "**it**" in the third paragraph refer to?

    (A) The study.   (B) Language.     (C) Roughness.     (D) The amygdala.

→ 答案為：(C)。因為掃讀後找出指涉題 it 所在的句子，接著在上一句裡找到 it 可能代替的兩個名詞 roughness (聲音的粗糙度) 和 language (語言)。將 roughness 和 language 代入所指涉的句子 but **it** is prevalent in artificial sounds 裡，判知 roughness (粗糙度) 的答案較合理。而且下一句也舉例說明鬧鐘、汽車喇叭及火災警報器三種人工聲音，皆具頗高的粗糙度，故可再次確認 it 所指涉的對象是 roughness。

( A ) 4. Which of the following devices may be improved with the researchers' findings?

此題判斷 inference

    (A) Smoke detectors.         (B) Security cameras.

    (C) Electric bug killers.      (D) Fire extinguishers.

範例二

    Is your dog an Einstein or a Charmer? For US $60, a recently-founded company called Dognition will help you learn more about your dog's cognitive traits. It offers an online test telling you about the brain behind the bark.

    Dognition's test measures a dog's intellect in several aspects—from empathy to memory to reasoning skills. But don't expect it to measure your pet's IQ. Dr. Hare, one of the venture's co-founders, says a dog's intelligence can't be described with a single number. Just as humans have a wide range of intelligences, so do dogs. The question is what type your dog relies on more.

After you plunk your money down, Dognition's website will take you through a questionnaire about your dog: For example, how excited does your dog get around other dogs, or children? Do fireworks scare your pup? Then, Dognition guides you through tests that are as fun as playing fetch or hide-and-seek. At the end, you get a report of your dog's cognitive profile.

Your dog could fall into one of nine categories: Ace, Stargazer, Maverick, Charmer, Socialite, Protodog, Einstein, Expert, or Renaissance Dog. That can give you something to brag about on Dognition's Facebook page. It also can shed new light on why dogs do the things they do. For example, a Charmer is a dog that trusts you so much that it would prefer to solve problems using information you give it rather than information it can get with its own eyes.

Dognition helps people understand their dogs in ways that they have never been able to do. This new understanding can enrich the relationship between dogs and their owners.

(106 學測)

( B ) 1. What is the third paragraph mainly about?　此題判斷 main idea

　　　(A) The theory behind the questionnaire used in the Dognition test.

　　　(B) The procedure for evaluating a dog's intellect on Dognition.

　　　(C) The products one can get by paying a fee to Dognition.

　　　(D) The characteristics of the activities Dognition offers.

( A ) 2. According to the passage, which of the following statements is true?　此題判斷 supporting details

　　　(A) Different dogs display strengths in different intelligences.

　　　(B) A dog's cognitive profile is composed of nine cognitive skills.

　　　(C) The purpose of Dognition's testing is to control a dog's behavior.

　　　(D) A dog's intelligence can be ranked based on the score of a Dognition's test.

( D ) 3. Which of the following is closest in meaning to the word "venture" in the second paragraph?　此題判斷 words in context

　　　(A) Creative measurement.　　　(B) Risky attempt.

　　　(C) Non-profit organization.　　　(D) New business.

( C ) 4. According to the passage, what would a Charmer most likely do?

　　(A) Stay away from people whenever possible.

　　(B) Imitate how other dogs solve problems.

　　(C) Rely on its owner to point out where a treat is.

　　(D) Follow its own senses to get what it wants.

→ 答案為：(C)。因為第四段的最後一句指出，"a Charmer is a dog that trusts you so much that it would prefer to solve problems using information you give it rather than information it can get with its own eyes." 可知迷人狗很信賴主人，因此寧願依賴主人所給的而非靠自己親眼所見的資訊來解決問題，可再次確認此推論正確。

## 實戰演練

請閱讀文章，並根據文章之文意為當題選出最適當的一個選項。

　　At first glance, a law establishing a minimum wage automatically benefits poorer members of society by making them more prosperous. They can be guaranteed a sufficient income to survive. Thus they can boost their national economy by using this money to buy products made by companies in their country. The taxes on their wages also help the government pay for services like healthcare and education.

　　On the other hand, some economists think **the situation is not so simple**. They claim that wage regulation interferes with natural economic processes, because labor is itself part of the market in a capitalist society. Workers' wages should therefore be like a price, reflecting the law of supply and demand, if capitalism is to work efficiently.

　　For example, if the economy is doing well, businesses will hire more staff and pay them more. If it is doing badly, wages will be reduced so that the companies can survive. A minimum wage would discourage employers from hiring when the economy is doing badly, because workers are too expensive. **This** would leave many out of work without a salary. In addition, it may encourage small businesses to use illegal labor at a lower wage. These workers would not pay taxes, so society would not benefit.

　　Nevertheless, viewed from another angle, this itself is a limited analysis. Treating wages as just another price ignores the human side of the question. Minimum wages should be regarded along the same lines as employees' safety. That is, as a social issue, not merely an economic one. In accordance with this attitude, a moderate solution would be to have a minimum wage but one that is not too low nor too high, so both employers and employees can mutually benefit.

此題判斷 reference

__B__ 1. Who does "**this**" in the third paragraph most likely refer to?
   (A) How businesses survive by paying staff more.
   (B) Expensive workers in bad economic times.
   (C) The trend to hire illegal labor at a lower wage.
   (D) Taxes collected from a minimum wage.

_____ 2. What does the sentence "**the situation is not so simple**" in the second paragraph imply?

此題判斷 _____

   (A) The existence of minimum wages will reflect the law of supply and demand and thus contribute to the advance of capitalism.
   (B) Wage regulation will yield greater productivity in natural economic processes, so businesses can hire fewer workers.
   (C) Benefits of labor, governments, and managements should all be taken into account when it comes to the issue of minimum wages.
   (D) The implementation of minimum wages will seriously reduce a country's competitiveness and decline its economic growth.

_____ 3. Which of the following can be inferred from the passage?

此題判斷 _____

   (A) Governments should take measures to boost national economy.
   (B) Minimum wages, labor and management will form a vicious circle.
   (C) Illegal labor is the biggest threat to full-time employees.
   (D) Lack of minimum wages might lead to various social problems.

_____ 4. What will the next paragraph discuss according to the last paragraph?

此題判斷 _____

   (A) Wage negotiations to benefit employers.
   (B) The rise and fall in minimum wages.
   (C) How to set a reasonable minimum wage.
   (D) The link between poverty and minimum wages.

閱讀完文章後，請針對下列問題用英文表達自己的想法與觀點。

1. A competition "Best Job in the World" pays a monthly wage of NT$1.5 million to hire someone as an ambassador to promote tourism in a tropical island for six months. Will you apply for it? Why or why not?

_____

_____

_____

_____

_____

2. In your view, do you agree to the establishment of a minimum wage? Why or why not? State your reasons.

_____

_____

_____

_____

_____

| Word Bank | |
| --- | --- |
| 1. minimum wage (n.) 最低工資 | 5. management (n.) 資方 |
| 2. healthcare (n.) 醫療保健 | 6. supply and demand (n.) 供需 |
| 3. capitalist (n.) 資本主義者<br>capitalism (n.) 資本主義 | 7. along the same lines as (phr.) 和…相同 |
| 4. labor (n.) 勞工；勞方 | 8. in accordance with (phr.) 依照 |

Acknowledgements:

The articles in this publication are adapted from the works by:

Ian Fletcher, Joseph E. Schier, Michael Ryan, Peter Wilds

Photo credits: Chris Jordan, ShutterStock

Babies are little scientists whose brains are structured very differently from adults. These young children are capable of learning much more than we previously believed and are reversing notions we once held about early learning. That's the conclusion of University of California, Berkeley psychologist Alison Gopnik, who has conducted extensive early childhood research during the past few years.

"Babies have many, many more neural connections being formed, many more synapses being formed, than we adults do," says Gopnik. "So it's as if early on, we have this brain that is really designed for learning, a brain that's very flexible and plastic and responds a lot to experiences. And then later on, as we get older, we have a brain that's more sort of a lean, mean machine, really designed to do things well, but not nearly as flexible, not nearly as good at learning something new."

When young children play with toys, they look very much like scientists doing experiments. They learn the way the world works through active observation, exploration, imagination, and experimentation. But many people equate "learning" with the type of teaching that traditionally occurs in school with the education of older children. They contend that children need to be taught how to learn by parents or teachers. Studies of young children playing, however, demonstrate that if children are "taught" a certain way to play with a toy, for example, they will imitate that action instead of experimenting on their own and consequently, learn less.

Based on her research, Gopnik maintains that we don't have to teach young children how to learn. Babies and young children are naturally curious and exploratory. We just need to love and care for them and allow them the opportunity to play without **interference**—learning will naturally follow.

下列四題請依據文章之文意選出最適當的一個選項。

_____ 1. Which of the following is the best title for the passage?

此題判斷 _____

(A) What Parents Should Know: Give Your Kid Advantages over Others

(B) Believe It or Not: Babies Are Natural and Creative Learners

(C) Teach Old Dogs New Tricks: An Impossible Mission

(D) Early Learning: The Secrets of Turning Babies into Psychologists.

_____ 2. According to the passage, babies do NOT excel in _____.

此題判斷 _____

(A) the number of neural connections and synapses

(B) the flexibility and quick response to the new stimulus

(C) the ability to do things well like a machine

(D) the potential for learning more new things

此題判斷 _____

_____ 3. What does the word "**interference**" in the last paragraph most likely refer to?

(A) Young kids' curiosity and exploratory abilities.

(B) Great love and infinite care from parents.

(C) Traditional school education and teaching methods.

(D) Parental instructions for kids on how to learn.

此題判斷 _____

_____ 4. If the author wants to share a successful case of early learning with readers in the next paragraph, which of the following examples will be mentioned?

(A) A mother teaches her son how to play with a new toy car and then he knows well how to copy her behavior.

(B) A father hires a super tutor to teach his 5-year-old daughter so that she can learn better due to such one-on-one attention.

(C) A mother gives her little child a lot of new toys and leaves him or her alone exploring how to play with them.

(D) A teacher offers pupils hands-on experiences by showing them how to conduct scientific experiments.

閱讀完文章後，請針對下列問題用英文表達自己的想法與觀點。

1. Gopnik contends that we don't need to teach young children, and learning will naturally occur. Do you think the same method can be applied to high school students like you? Why or why not?

_____

_____

_____

2. The following is the popular "Learning Pyramid" theory, which proposes that students can have the highest retention rate (as high as 90%) by teaching others. That is, they can remember what they have learned longer and better if they teach others how to do it. Do you agree or not? Provide your personal experience to support your ideas.

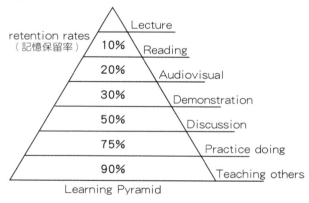

retention rates（記憶保留率）
- 10% Lecture
- Reading
- 20% Audiovisual
- 30% Demonstration
- 50% Discussion
- 75% Practice doing
- 90% Teaching others

Learning Pyramid

_____

_____

_____

### Word Bank

1. extensive (adj.) 大量的；大規模的
2. neural (adj.) 神經的
3. synapse (n.) 突觸；神經鍵
   （兩個神經細胞的相接處）
4. plastic (adj.) 可塑性高的；易受影響的
5. lean, mean machine (n.) 精實出色的機器

6. experimentation (n.) 實驗法
7. equate (v.) 使相等；使等同
8. contend (v.) 堅決主張；聲稱
9. exploratory (adj.) 探究的
10. interference (n.) 干預；干涉

The Industrial Revolution of the 19th century changed a lot. What was once made by hand could be automated with the use of machines. Things were made faster and cheaper, but with this increase in productivity came a new problem. Many low-skilled workers found themselves out of work. The same happened with the arrival of computers which further increased automation.

Still, there are many jobs a machine could never do, right? Think again. Even now there are robots filling customer service roles in Japan. The Henn-na Hotel, for instance, is staffed entirely by robots. These robots are made to look like people, have moving limbs and can make facial expressions. They are able to greet customers, answer questions in multiple languages and even order taxis. While they can't have proper conversations with people yet, they are rapidly becoming more **sophisticated**. Who knows what's around the corner?

Is this the beginning of another era of technological change? That remains to be seen. These robots may look like people, but they can't think like us. True robots would require artificial intelligence which is still a long way off from being fully realized.

This hasn't stopped people from wondering what a society fully automated by robots would be like though. Some believe that the majority of non-professionals will be left out as they would be unable to provide value to the rich and powerful. How would most people make a living if they aren't needed to work in factories, make coffee or drive taxis? Both the industrial and information ages prompted the same predictions, but this new technology actually created more jobs than it took away, and with the increased production, it has raised the standard of living for everyone.

下列四題請依據文章之文意選出最適當的一個選項。

_____ 1. Which of the following is NOT mentioned in the passage as one of the changes brought about by the Industrial Revolution?

此題判斷 _____

(A) Automation.
(B) Healthcare.
(C) Productivity.
(D) Unemployment.

_____ 2. Why does the author mention robots in the second paragraph?

此題判斷 _____

(A) To replace all customer service agents with robots in the world.
(B) To introduce the human-like robots in Japan's Henn-na Hotel.
(C) To suggest the possibility that robots will change the job market.
(D) To develop robots with better language and conversation abilities.

_____ 3. What does the word "**sophisticated**" in the second paragraph most likely mean?

此題判斷 _____

(A) Artificial and professional.
(B) Elegant and fashionable.
(C) Automatic and labor-saving.
(D) More advanced and complex.

_____ 4. What will the next paragraph discuss according to the last paragraph?

此題判斷 _____

(A) How the replacement for unskilled jobs will contribute to income inequality.
(B) An extensive investigation into the number of unemployed people in search of new jobs.
(C) The introduction of new fields and potential jobs for people in the coming robotic age.
(D) The influence of artificial intelligence and machine learning on the future robotic development.

閱讀完文章後，請針對下列問題用英文表達自己的想法與觀點。

1. If possible, do you want to stay in a robot-staffed hotel? Why or why not? State your reasons.

_____

_____

_____

_____

2. In your opinion, what are some jobs that won't be replaced by robots in the future?

_____

_____

_____

_____

## Word Bank

1. automate (v.) 使自動化
   automation (n.) 自動化

2. productivity (n.) 生產力

3. out of work (adj.) 失業

4. fill (v.) 填補…的空缺

5. facial expression (n.) 臉部表情

6. sophisticated (adj.) (機器) 複雜精密的；
   高度發展的

7. around the corner (adj.) 即將來臨

8. era (n.) 時代

9. artificial intelligence (n.) 人工智慧

10. non-professional (n.) 無專業技能者，
    非專家，外行者

11. leave out (v.) 除去，省去

12. prompt (v.) 引起，激起

A webcast is a media presentation broadcast over the Internet. Originally, they were designed for entertainment purposes. The first, produced by Apple in 1995, was an audio webcast of concerts in New York clubs. The standard audio plus video webcast soon developed and rock bands used them to broadcast live concerts on the Internet.

Since then, webcasting has grown into a global phenomenon. Professional webcasting is much cheaper than traditional TV broadcasting which uses satellites. Therefore, people can afford to pay fees for webcasting services for events such as weddings. Nowadays, ordinary people can use free technology to make webcasts from home. In Korea, for example, an attractive woman has become famous for webcasts of herself eating. While she eats, she chats with viewers and is able to make a living from her fans' contributions.

Webcasting has also become a major feature of business. Companies use it to broadcast conferences, meetings and training videos to employees anywhere in the world. Others use this technology for marketing and sales. In addition, webcasting has also greatly affected education. Many professional organizations will advertise webcasts on special subjects and viewers pay to watch the webcast given by an expert. Universities use webcasts for lectures, and **these** are especially common for online courses, taken by millions of people.

People tend to regard webcasting as a phenomenon limited to the present in real time. However, although webcasts may be often purely live events, many are now recorded and saved. The US Library of Congress, the largest in the world, has thousands of webcasts on various subjects. Thus webcasting is likely to make an important contribution to the store of human knowledge for future generations.

### ⏱ 實戰演練

下列四題請依據文章之文意選出最適當的一個選項。

_____ 1. What is the third paragraph mainly about?　　　此題判斷 _____

　　(A) The history and current development of the webcasting services.

　　(B) Why professional webcasting has become a global phenomenon.

　　(C) How various industries can benefit from webcasting technologies.

　　(D) The interactivity tools and management required by webcasting.

_____ 2. What does "**these**" in the third paragraph most likely refer to?

此題判斷 _____

　　(A) Viewers.　　　(B) Universities.　　(C) Lectures.　　(D) Webcasts.

_____ 3. According to the passage, which of the following is NOT a suitable description of webcasting?

此題判斷 _____

　　(A) The first audio plus video webcast was developed by Apple in 1995.

　　(B) Free technology has much to do with the popularity of webcasting.

　　(C) Now ordinary people can produce webcasts and share them online.

　　(D) Webcasts can be watched both live and non-real time on the Internet.

_____ 4. From the passage, it can be inferred that webcasting is now _____ to the general public than other media presentations.

此題判斷 _____

　　(A) less entertaining (B) more appealing　(C) less accessible　(D) more complex

## ✏️ 回答問題

閱讀完文章後，請針對下列問題用英文表達自己的想法與觀點。

1. Have you watched webcasts online? Share your experience. If not, will you try it? Why or why not?

_____

_____

_____

2. Will you consider taking online webcast courses? Why or why not?

_____

_____

_____

| Word Bank | |
|---|---|
| 1. webcast (n./v.) 網路直播 | 5. marketing (n.) 行銷 |
| 2. audio (adj.) 聲音的 | 6. online course (n.) 線上課程 |
| 3. satellite (n.) 衛星 | 7. real time (n.) 即時 |
| 4. contribution (n.) 捐助；貢獻 | 8. The US Library of Congress 美國國會圖書館 |

To a person who observes the tides, seawater appears to be pulled backward at low tide, and then pushed forward at high tide along the water's horizontal line.

In fact, the pull is vertical. The moon exerts gravity from above, so water directly underneath it is actually dragged upward into a **bulge**. This forms the high tides in regions directly below the moon. Quite a few people conclude that water on the earth's opposite side should also move upward to the same extent, thus creating low tides there. However, this is not an accurate inference. The lunar gravity pulls both the solid earth toward the moon and water in and around the upper bulge. Its force is weakest on water at the earth's opposite end, so the water there remains and forms a bulge, creating another high tide. Low tides therefore form at the sides of the vertical line of moon and earth.

The earth rotating on its axis once a day causes the phenomenon of two daily tides. Low tides in an area occur as the earth turns away from being directly underneath the moon. High tides return approximately twelve hours later when the area is again under the moon, but this time with the mass of the earth between them. In another twelve hours, the area will again be directly under the moon with only the atmosphere between them.

Tides were important to our ancestors. Fishermen discovered that fish gathered in greater numbers when the tide was ebbing. This enabled them to fish more efficiently at these times. Moreover, tides are likely to play an important part in mankind's future. They could be a major source of clean renewable energy. Tidal power stations use the tidal movements to rotate turbines that convert the force of the water into electricity.

### ⏱ 實戰演練

下列四題請依據文章之文意選出最適當的一個選項。

_____ 1. What is the purpose of this passage?　　　　此題判斷 _____

　(A) To discuss the necessity of tidal observations.

　(B) To raise doubts about the theory of tidal formation.

　(C) To introduce tides and their importance to earth.

　(D) To emphasize the use of tidal power on underwater turbines.

2. Which of the following picture matches the formation of tides described in the second paragraph?

此題判斷 _____

(A)

high tide

low tide Earth low tide Moon

high tide

(B)

low tide

low tide Earth high tide Moon

high tide

(C)

high tide

high tide Earth low tide Moon

low tide

(D)

low tide

high tide Earth high tide Moon

low tide

3. According to the passage, which of the following statements is true?

此題判斷 _____

(A) When an area on earth turns away from being directly under the moon, high tides occur.

(B) The moon's gravity pulls seawater horizontally rather than vertically.

(C) The mass of the earth is always between the tide and the moon when the two daily high tides return.

(D) Fishermen can easily catch fish at low tides, when fish gather together.

4. According to the second paragraph, what is a "**bulge**?"

此題判斷 _____

(A) A region below the moon.   (B) The moon's gravity.

(C) The water's vertical line.   (D) A high tide.

## ✎ 回答問題

閱讀完文章後，請針對下列問題用英文表達自己的想法與觀點。

1. The following are quotes about "tides." Which do you like the most? Why?

· Time and tide wait for no one.

· Take charge of your life! The tides do not command the ship. The sailor does.

· The captain of a ship can run a great ship, but he/she can't do anything about the tides.

- Life is like the sea. Its tides and currents sometimes take a person to distant shores that he/she never dreamed existed.
- The lowest ebb is the turn of the tide.

_____

_____

2. Your best friend Carl sent a LINE message to you and invited you to watch tidal waves before the typhoon comes. As his best friend, how will you **discourage** him from doing such a dangerous and life-risking activity? Read the message below and reply to it.

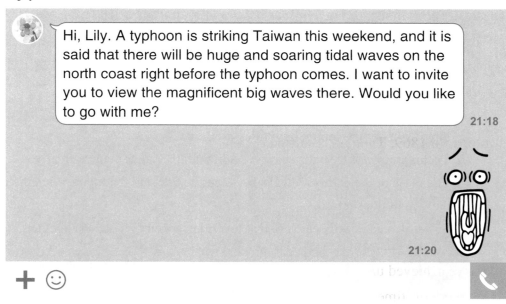

Hi, Lily. A typhoon is striking Taiwan this weekend, and it is said that there will be huge and soaring tidal waves on the north coast right before the typhoon comes. I want to invite you to view the magnificent big waves there. Would you like to go with me?

21:18

21:20

_____

_____

| Word Bank | |
| --- | --- |
| 1. horizontal (adj.) 水平的 | 6. rotate (v.) 轉動 (尤指圍繞定點) |
| 2. vertical (adj.) 垂直的 | 7. axis (n.) 地軸；軸 (線) |
| 3. exert (v.) 施加 (影響) | 8. ebb (v.) 退 (潮) |
| 4. inference (n.) 推論 | 9. renewable energy (n.) 再生能源 |
| 5. tidal bulge (n.) 潮汐隆起；隆堆 | 10. turbine (n.) 渦輪機 |

In the ancient Egyptian writing system, the "ankh" character means "life." It consists of a long vertical line with a shorter horizontal line across the top end. Resting on the latter is a circular shape which is pointed as it joins it.

However, the ankh is also an important symbol in ancient Egyptian culture, and can exist as an independent physical object. For example, statues of many Egyptian gods and pharaohs have the figures holding ankhs. Archaeologists discovered thousands of ankhs when they dug up royal tombs in the nineteenth and twentieth centuries. The ankh was frequently carved on the doorways of tombs. Inside the burial chambers they would be found in the decorations and wall paintings. The famous coffin of Queen Ahmose-Nefertari has the queen's figure with arms crossed over the chest, holding an ankh in each hand. The ankh was supposed to help the dead on their journey to the afterlife, providing a link between the mortal and eternal realms.

No sooner had the ankh sign been discovered than scholars began researching its origins. In 1869, Thomas Inman suggested that, because it meant "life," it was a representation of the male and female sexual organs. The lines were the male's and the circular shape the female's. Others thought this was nonsense and proposed various theories. For instance, one thought it was a belt buckle of the mother goddess, Isis, another that it showed the sun rising above the horizon. None have achieved universal acceptance among contemporary scholars.

In modern times the ankh has been adopted by "New Age" spiritual movements as a symbol of power and wisdom, and it survives as a common design in jewelry such as necklaces. Nevertheless, the actual origin of the ankh still remains a mystery, **obscured** by the mists of time.

下列四題請依據文章之文意選出最適當的一個選項。

_____ 1. According to the first paragraph, which of the following might be the "ankh" in the ancient Egyptian writing system?　　此題判斷 _____

(A) 　(B) 　(C) 　(D)

_____ 2. According to the passage, which of the following statements is NOT true regarding the ankh?　　此題判斷 _____

(A) The ankh serves as spiritual symbols of life rather than physical objects.

(B) The ankh can be found in statues, wall paintings, as well as coffins.

(C) The dead hold ankhs to secure their journey to the life after death.

(D) The circular shape of ankhs represents the female's sexual organ.

_____ 3. What is the third paragraph mainly about?　　此題判斷 _____

(A) The developments of the ankh sign in Egyptian history.

(B) The functions of the ankh sign in religious occasions.

(C) The different theories about the origins of the ankh sign.

(D) The academic studies on the ankh sign by foreign researchers.

_____ 4. Which of the following is closest in meaning to "**obscured**" in the last paragraph?　　此題判斷 _____

(A) Made difficult to understand.　　(B) Forced to give up.

(C) Kept alive to ensure freshness.　　(D) Found to last long.

閱讀完文章後，請針對下列問題用英文表達自己的想法與觀點。

1. Do you believe in afterlife? Why or why not? State your reasons.

_____

_____

2. Your brother is going to take an important entrance exam. Which of the following symbols will you choose as a lucky charm to give him a sense of inner peace and wish him good luck? Why?

| A | B | C | D | E | F Others |
|---|---|---|---|---|---|
| | | | | | |

_____

_____

## Word Bank

1. ankh (n.) 古埃及十字架 ；生命之符 (頂上有圓環，是生命的象徵)
2. pharaoh (n.) 埃及法老
3. archaeologist (n.) 考古學家
4. doorway (n.) 門口；出入口
5. burial chamber (n.) 墓室
6. coffin (n.) 棺材；靈柩
7. afterlife (n.) 來世
8. eternal (adj.) 永恆的；不朽的
9. realm (n.) 界；領域
10. sexual organ (n.) 性器官
11. nonsense (n.) 胡說；無稽之談
12. belt buckle (n.) 皮帶扣
13. Isis (n.) 埃及司農業及受胎之女神
14. the New Age Movement (n.) 新時代運動 (1970～80 年西方社會運動)
15. obscure (v.) 使難以理解；遮掩

In Japan, otaku was typically an offensive term meaning nerd or geek. Nowadays, many Japanese have embraced the label and it is no longer considered negative. It describes a fan or someone whose identity is significantly defined by a specific hobby, such as anime, manga and video games. Outside of Japan, otaku can refer to those not only interested in Japanese cartoons and comics but obsessed with Japanese culture in general.

The usage of the word "otaku" began in the 1980s and coincides with the surge in popularity of anime at the time. It represented a subculture of social **outcasts** who could not raise their social status through athletic or academic success and so instead focused on other interests. The notion of an otaku was of a socially awkward and troubled person, living an isolated life, killing time watching anime and reading manga. The label became even more negative after Tsutomu Miyazaki, an otaku, was found to have killed four young girls. He was later called the "Otaku Murderer." Fortunately, otaku's bad reputation has faded and the definition has also changed to represent people involved in fandoms. Nowadays, 42% of Japanese are identified as a type of otaku.

Otaku generally focus on a specific fandom or genre of anime, manga, video games, cosplay and others. Anime and manga are Japanese forms of animation and comic media respectively and are the major interests of most otaku.

These days, the Akihabara District in Tokyo is the center of otaku culture and contains many shops for anime and manga products as well as maid and other themed cafés. In maid cafés, waitresses are dressed in maid costumes similar to those featured in manga. Other cafés revolve around a theme based on an anime or manga. In these cafés, customers are encouraged to dress up as their favorite characters.

Otaku have not only had to overcome the personal issues that lead them to this lifestyle, but also the panic and suspicion of the public as a whole. In spite of its troubled past, otaku culture is flourishing in Japan as well as internationally.

下列四題請依據文章之文意選出最適當的一個選項。

_____ 1. According to the passage, which of the following statements is true about Japan's otaku culture?　　此題判斷 _____

　　(A) It was originally a positive term praising people for their academic success.

　　(B) Television and shopping addicts can be defined as a typical otaku.

　　(C) The popularity of anime fostered Japan's otaku culture.

　　(D) A lone otaku can raise his social status by watching anime.

_____ 2. What is the second paragraph mainly about?　　此題判斷 _____

　　(A) The analysis of different Japanese subcultures.

　　(B) Rising crime rates and the popularity of Japanese anime.

　　(C) The history and development of the otaku culture.

　　(D) Differences between men and women otaku fandoms.

_____ 3. What does the word "**outcasts**" in the second paragraph most likely refer to?　　此題判斷 _____

　　(A) People who focus on their athletic or academic success.

　　(B) People who carry a negative label of killing young girls.

　　(C) People who are fond of watching anime and reading manga

　　(D) People who are unwanted and alone in a certain group.

_____ 4. Which of the following statements is true according to the passage?　　此題判斷 _____

　　(A) Video games and cosplay are two major interests of most otaku in Japan.

　　(B) With many anime and manga shops, Osaka is the otaku landmark in Japan.

　　(C) In maid cafés, otaku are encouraged to dress in maid costumes.

　　(D) Public panic and suspicion do not stop the spread of otaku culture.

閱讀完文章後，請針對下列問題用英文表達自己的想法與觀點。

1. Are you involved in a specific fandom of something (like detective novels, railway, science fiction, anime and manga, comics, sports, music, soap operas, celebrities, video games, etc.)? Why or why not? Please explain.

_____

_____

_____

2. If you are given a chance to dine in maid cafés or in restaurants of different themes based on anime or manga, will you try it? Why or why not?

_____

_____

_____

_____

| Word Bank | |
|---|---|
| 1. otaku (n.) 御宅族；宅男 | 8. surge (n.) 激增 |
| 2. nerd (n.) 書呆子、電腦迷 | 9. subculture (n.) 次文化 (社會中某個人群特有的) |
| 3. geek (n.) 怪咖；理工科宅男；土包子 | 10. outcast (n.) 被社會或團體拋棄或排擠的人 |
| 4. anime (n.) 日本動畫 | 11. notion (n.) 概念；想法 |
| 5. manga (n.) 日本連環漫畫 | 12. fandom (n.) 狂熱的…迷；…熱 |
| 6. be obsessed with (v.) 對…著迷 | 13. cosplay (n.) 角色扮演 |
| 7. coincide with sth (v.) 與…同時發生 | 14. maid cafeé (n.) 女僕咖啡廳 |

When different wavelengths of light enter our eyes, we perceive different colors. Objects will reflect and absorb specific wavelengths and therefore have a color. Color theories attempt to organize colors in a logical way and determine how they interact and mix with each other. Colors that originate from light sources, such as TVs, follow different rules from colors that come from paints and dyes. As light is mixed together, the color will eventually become white. In contrast, when many paints are mixed, the color will become black. Knowledge of color theories is important for artists as they use a limited set of paints to create a wide range of hues.

The historical foundation of color theory is based on the red, yellow and blue color model. These colors were considered the "primary colors," from which all other colors were made. When two of these colors are mixed, a secondary color is produced: green, orange or purple. For instance, yellow turns into green when combined with blue. When a primary is mixed with a secondary, **a tertiary color** is created. Tertiary colors have a two-colored name, such as yellow-orange. Arranging these colors logically in a circle forms what is called a color wheel. Sir Isaac Newton developed the first color wheel in the 17th century. Nowadays, we understand that other models of primary colors can be used, such as magenta, yellow and cyan in printing and red, blue and green for monitors.

Color harmony is a combination of colors viewed as pleasing and is based on the color wheel. There are many types of harmonious color combinations, one of them being two complimentary colors, which are colors that are opposite each other on the color wheel. Complimentary colors, such as red and green, when put together, create the highest contrast and therefore stand out. Another harmony is when three or more colors next to each other on the color wheel make up a composition.

To be a successful painter, knowledge of how to create the exact color you want is essential. And knowing how colors harmoniously interact with each other is required to make an impressive work, which is why color theory is important for any artist or designer.

下列四題請依據文章之文意選出最適當的一個選項。

_____ 1. What is the passage mainly about?　此題判斷 _____

(A) The origins of color theory and the development of the color wheel.

(B) The introduction of color theory and its importance to art professionals.

(C) The knowledge of different color models and its application to the market.

(D) The tips on creating impressive art works based on classical color theory.

_____ 2. Which of the following statements about colors is true?　此題判斷 _____

(A) People see colors because they organize colors based on color theories.

(B) If we mix different light together, we will get the color black.

(C) When colors are arranged logically in a circle, they form a color wheel.

(D) The primary colors for monitors are magenta, yellow, and cyan.

_____ 3. According to the passage, what are "**tertiary colors**"?　此題判斷 _____

(A) They are red, yellow, and blue, which form the tertiary color model.

(B) They can create a secondary color when two of them are mixed.

(C) When they are mixed with a primary color, a secondary color is created.

(D) They are two-named colors, such as blue-purple, red-orange, etc.

_____ 4. What do we know about color harmony from the passage?　此題判斷 _____

(A) It can be described as an arrangement of colors that goes well together and is pleasing to the eyes.

(B) It may occur when three or more colors directly opposite each other on the color wheel.

(C) Any two complimentary colors side by side on the color wheel can be put together to create harmony.

(D) Color combinations that have the highest contrast and stand out are not examples of color harmony.

閱讀完文章後，請針對下列問題用英文表達自己的想法與觀點。

1. What is your favorite color? Why do you like it so much? Provide your reasons.

_____

_____

_____

_____

2. Can you imagine a world only with black and white? What our world would be like without the other colors? Try to imagine that and explain the advantages or disadvantages of such a colorless world.

_____

_____

_____

_____

### Word Bank

1. wavelength (n.) 波長
2. hue (n.) 顏色；色彩；色相
3. primary colors (n.) 原色；基色
   (即紅、黃、藍色)
4. secondary color (n.) 第二次色；間色 (由相鄰的原色混合而成。如：紅＋黃＝橘)
5. tertiary color (n.) 第三次色；複色 (由原色跟相鄰的間色混合而成。如：黃＋橘＝黃橘)
6. a color wheel (n.) 色環
7. magenta (n.) 洋紅色
8. cyan (n.) 青色 (印刷術語)
9. color harmony (n.) 色彩調和
10. complimentary color (n.) 互補色

The ancient Greeks established medicine as a separate science. Their physicians also considered medical ethics, developing a written code of conduct. This became known as the Hippocratic Oath, named after Hippocrates, one of the Greek founders of scientific medicine.

The oath required doctors to respect patients' dignity, promising to never harm a patient, and to only recommend healthy diets. They also had to refuse medicine to end a patient's life even if asked for. In addition, they swore never to give medicine to "any pregnant woman with a view to destroying the child."

After the Dark Ages, Greek medicine was rediscovered, contributing to the development of modern medical science. In the sixteenth century, some famous schools began to employ the oath at their graduation ceremonies. It has been respected for centuries as a guide to doctors' moral responsibilities.

However, in the twentieth century, its rules seemed too rigid for certain complex issues regarding the taking of human life. Nowadays, ending a pregnancy is legal in some circumstances, for example if a baby will be born diseased. Furthermore, there is a trend toward physician-assisted suicide, such as when a patient has a terminal illness with great suffering. In both cases, allowing a medical professional to end a life is recognized as a compassionate option.

Consequently, modified versions of the Hippocratic Oath were composed. The one most used today was written in 1964 by the Dean of the School of Medicine at Tufts University. It honors the original ideas of respect and compassion for patients, but doctors now swear "**It may also be in my power to take a life.**" The new oath forms a part of medical ethics courses in universities around the world. It reflects how ideas about doctors' duties have changed over time, but what it retains shows the extent to which we are still influenced by the ancient Greeks.

下列四題請依據文章之文意選出最適當的一個選項。

_____ 1. What can we learn from this passage?　　此題判斷 _____

(A) How Greek medicine evolves into a separate science.

(B) How the Hippocratic Oath is employed at graduation ceremonies.

(C) Medical ethics and doctor's moral responsibilities may change over time.

(D) The taking of any human life should be considered a compassionate option.

_____ 2. According to the passage, _____ is part of the　　此題判斷 _____ original Hippocratic Oath.

(A) showing respect for patients' social status

(B) giving advice on patients' diets

(C) ending a woman's pregnancy

(D) performing physician-assisted suicide

此題判斷 _____

_____ 3. Which of the following statements is NOT true according to the passage?

(A) The development of the Hippocratic Oath is introduced in time order.

(B) Both scientific medicine and the Hippocratic Oath originated in ancient Greece.

(C) Abortion for serious birth defects is allowed in today's medical practice.

(D) Compassion is excluded from the modified version of the Hippocratic Oath.

_____ 4. What does the sentence "**It may also be in my power to take a life**" in the last paragraph imply?

此題判斷 _____

(A) The modified version of the Hippocratic Oath seems too rigid for doctors.

(B) Doctors nowadays are allowed to terminate a patient's life if necessary.

(C) The power and status of doctors have been improved in modern society.

(D) Medical ethics courses should be made a required subject in medical schools.

閱讀完文章後，請針對下列問題用英文表達自己的想法與觀點。

1. In your opinion, are you for or against "physician-assisted suicide"? Why? State your reasons.

_____

_____

_____

_____

2. Recently, a rise in violent attacks on Emergency Room (ER) doctors and nurses has hit newspaper headlines. What is your opinion about ER violence?

_____

_____

_____

_____

## Word Bank

1. physician (n.) 醫生；內科醫生
2. medical ethics (n.) 醫學倫理
3. code of conduct (n.) 行為準則
4. the Hippocratic Oath (n.) 希波克拉底誓詞；醫師誓詞
5. rigid (adj.) 嚴格的；死板的
6. physician-assisted suicide (n.) 醫助自殺
7. terminal (adj.) 末期的
8. compassionate (adj.) 慈悲的；憐憫的
9. modified (adj.) 修改的

A county in central England has become the first in the country to combat misogyny against women by making it a hate crime. Nottinghamshire is defining misogynistic hate crimes as "incidents against women that are motivated by an attitude of a man toward a woman, and includes behavior targeted toward a woman by men simply because they are a woman." Such hate crimes include conduct such as verbal and physical abuse, harassment on the street, sexual advances, and the uses of mobile phones to send messages or take pictures without women's consent beforehand.

Nottinghamshire joins several other European nations, including Belgium and Portugal, which have made misogyny, including verbal abuse, a hate crime. The law in Belgium was passed after a female filmmaker used a hidden camera to record comments made to her while walking down the street.

A national coalition of women's organizations in Great Britain published its 2016 study indicating that 85% of British women aged 18–24 had experienced "unwanted sexual attention in public places" and felt it necessary to do "**safety planning**" before going out at night to protect themselves. More than half of the women surveyed said they feel unsafe in public places.

Sarah Green, Acting Director of the End Violence Against Women Coalition, commented: "We did this survey to find out about the scale of sexual harassment and the impact it has on the way women live. If women are planning their lives around not being harassed or assaulted, they are not free. Women should be free to live their lives without the threat of harassment and violence, not having to plan and limit their choices to make sure they're safe."

Nottinghamshire women are applauding the law as a significant step to broaden the definition of hate crimes to include all forms of misogyny. They are hopeful the new law will result in Nottinghamshire being a safer place to live in.

下列四題請依據文章之文意選出最適當的一個選項。

_____ 1. What is the passage mainly about?

此題判斷 _____

(A) The definition of misogyny and hate crimes.

(B) A new British law to increase safety of women.

(C) Women's rights and social status in Nottinghamshire.

(D) The threat of harassment and violence facing women.

_____ 2. According to the passage, which of the following statements is true regarding misogynistic hate crimes?

此題判斷 _____

(A) Nottinghamshire is the last English county to pass the law relating to misogynistic hate crimes.

(B) They occur when a female adopts a hostile attitude toward a male sexist.

(C) Currently, only three European regions have made misogyny a hate crime.

(D) Using a hidden camera to photograph pretty women on the street is not against the law.

_____ 3. What is implied about "**safety planning**" in the passage?

此題判斷 _____

(A) Safety planning is only required by young women aged 18–24.

(B) Less than 50% of British women need it due to undesired sexual attention.

(C) All women's organizations in England are calling for safety planning.

(D) The safer a city is, the less likely women are to do safety planning.

_____ 4. The author's tone in this passage is best described as _____.

此題判斷 _____

(A) negative

(B) emotional

(C) objective

(D) critical

閱讀完文章後，請針對下列問題用英文表達自己的想法與觀點。

1. Do you agree to make misogyny a hate crime? Why or why not?

_____

_____

_____

_____

_____

2. Do you think Taiwan is a safe place for women to live in? Why or why not?

_____

_____

_____

_____

_____

## Word Bank

1. combat (v.) 打擊；制止

2. misogyny (n.) 厭惡女性；女性貶抑
   misogynistic (adj.) 厭惡女性的

3. hate crime (n.) (對同性戀者、有色種族或少數民族等的) 仇恨犯罪；仇視犯罪

4. verbal abuse (n.) 口語暴力
   physical abuse (n.) 肢體暴力

5. harassment (n.) 騷擾
   harass (v.) 騷擾

6. sexual advances (n. pl.) 性挑逗

7. consent (n.) 同意；贊成

8. beforehand (adv.) 事先；預先

9. coalition (n.) 聯盟；同盟

10. sexual attention (n.) 性關注

11. safety planning (n.) 安全計畫

12. assault (v.) 攻擊

13. applaud (v.) 贊成；喝采

Picture yourself waiting in line at a bank or riding the subway to work. If you were to describe the people around you, what activity do you think they would be doing? Probably the first thing that comes to mind these days is that the people would be staring at their smartphones. Maybe they are playing games, sending text messages, or just surfing the Internet. Whatever it is they are doing, they are certainly killing time in what normally would be considered a boring situation.

A lot of people hail using smartphone as the easiest way to get rid of all the little boring times that litter our lives. However, this may not be a good thing. In fact, doing away with all that boredom can actually have a **detrimental** effect on your lives. While you may not find boredom all that enjoyable, periods of boredom are actually good for your brains.

Rather than being something that should be avoided at all costs, boredom can actually be a gift. In a world where humans are bombarded by advertising, news, and so many other distractions, it is surprising that many people choose to become further distracted by constantly looking at the smartphones. Some argue that people should not do that but instead embrace boredom as a time when the brains are able to work with a blank slate. Instead of occupying the minds with the stimulation provided by the smartphones, people should allow their minds to wander. This type of mind wandering allows humans to explore the imagination and let the creative juices start flowing once again.

There are plenty of instances where great ideas have come about after periods of boredom. When these times happen, people usually call it daydreaming. If we take daydreaming out of the equation because we are always kept focused on our smartphones, isn't it fair to say that we are losing something?

Next time you're riding the bus or waiting in line for tickets, leave your smartphone in your pocket. Let boredom set in for a bit; it might lead you to a place that's surprisingly wonderful!

下列四題請依據文章之文意選出最適當的一個選項。

_____ 1. Which of the following sentences best states the main idea of the passage?

此題判斷 _____

(A) The invention of smartphones signals the end of humans' boredom.

(B) Boredom is the root of all evil and the source of endless mental torture.

(C) Boredom is an intellectual defeat that leads to fear and loneliness.

(D) Boredom promotes imagination and a period of great creativity.

_____ 2. Which of the following is closest in meaning to "**detrimental**" in the second paragraph?

此題判斷 _____

(A) Various.　　　　　　　(B) Distracted.

(C) Harmful.　　　　　　　(D) Inevitable.

_____ 3. According to the passage, which of the following statements is true?

此題判斷 _____

(A) Technologies help combat people's boredom by offering distractions anywhere and anytime.

(B) Phubbing (低頭滑手機) the smartphone and watching news enable our brain to work with a blank slate.

(C) Daydreaming and mind wandering provide a lot of stimulation that occupies our minds.

(D) Boredom is a curse for writers and artists, which prevents them from creating wonderful works.

_____ 4. What is the author's attitude toward boredom in this passage?

此題判斷 _____

(A) Mocking.　　　　　　　(B) Encouraging.

(C) Indifferent.　　　　　　(D) Sympathetic.

## 回答問題

閱讀完文章後，請針對下列問題用英文表達自己的想法與觀點。

1. Look at the following picture. Why did Kelly look so bored last Friday? How did she combat her boredom? Last, what do you think would happen to Kelly in the end?

_____

_____

_____

2. In your opinion, the invention of smartphones has changed our lives for the better or worse? Why? State your reasons.

_____

_____

_____

| Word Bank |
|---|

1. hail sb/sth as sth (v.) 讚揚⋯為⋯

2. litter (v.) 充滿

3. do away with (v.) 廢除；停止

4. detrimental (adj.) 不利的；有害的

5. at all costs (adv.) 無論如何；不計代價

6. bombard sb/sth with sth (v.) 轟炸

7. distraction (n.) 令人分心的事物
   distract (v.) 使分心

8. blank slate (n.) 空白板

9. come about (v.) 發生

10. equation (n.) 含多種因素的平衡；綜合體；等式

11. set in (v.) 到來；開始流動

12. phub (v.) 滑手機
    (=phone 手機 + snub 冷落)
    phubber (n.) 低頭族

The "uni" in "universe" comes from the Latin for "one." Until recent decade the word, invented in the 1580s with the rise of modern science, seemed an appropriate choice. A single physical universe was said to have emerged from the primary explosion known as the Big Bang. It is also reported to be expanding over light speed, so instruments will never be able to see its frontiers. Although this aroused awe, it was comforting that the universe telescopes observed had the four familiar dimensions, operating in time and space.

However, it just so happens that this model now appears totally mistaken. In the 1980s, discoveries in the realm of astronomy provided support for a revolutionary new theory. The findings were so extraordinary that language itself had to change to describe them. Scientists needed to remove the "uni" from "universe."

When astronomers measured the amount of gravity created at the Big Bang, the data revealed something extraordinary. **It** indicated a quantity of gravity vastly larger than what exists in the observed universe. So where did all this extra gravity disappear into? The logical explanation was that there were numerous expansions from the initial event, creating perhaps an infinite number of other worlds. Furthermore, these might have bizarre characteristics beyond anything we can conceive of.

Consequently, the word "multiverse" became a feature of scientific vocabulary. "Multi" means "many" in Latin, as in the word "multiple," and thus seems to match the actual circumstances. This new complexity exposes the limitations of knowledge. We are unable to even observe the end of our own universe, so it is impossible to explore these remote creations. We simply know they are probably out there, somewhere. Nevertheless, most of us still use the traditional term "universe," perhaps because these worlds beyond worlds are too much for our minds to constantly contemplate. As the poet T.S. Eliot wrote, **"Human kind cannot bear very much reality."**

下列四題請依據文章之文意選出最適當的一個選項。

_____ 1. According to the passage, which of the following statements is true?　此題判斷 _____

　(A) New discoveries in biology in the 1580s helped invent the word "universe."

　(B) The universe emerged from the primary explosion, the Big Bang.

　(C) The universe expanding at light speed is observable with telescopes.

　(D) Our universe had four dimensions, which operated in space only.

_____ 2. What does the word "**It**" in the third paragraph most likely refer to?　此題判斷 _____

　(A) A large quantity of strong gravity measured by astronomers at the Big Bang.

　(B) The detailed data revealed by astronomers about the rise of modern science.

　(C) The explanation for the bizarre characteristics of the physical universe.

　(D) A finding about an extra amount of gravity created by the Big Bang.

_____ 3. Why do scientists have to take the "uni" away from the word "universe?"　此題判斷 _____

　(A) To reflect the trend toward the invention of new scientific vocabulary.

　(B) To offer people understanding about unknown space creatures.

　(C) To support a new theory that there might be countless other worlds.

　(D) To measure the universe's extra gravity and find out where it disappeared to.

_____ 4. Where does this passage most likely appear?　此題判斷 _____

　(A) In a science magazine.　　(B) In a travel guide.

　(C) In a biology textbook.　　(D) In a business journal.

閱讀完文章後，請針對下列問題用英文表達自己的想法與觀點。

1. Do you believe in the existence of aliens? If so, what do they look like? Please explain.

_____

_____

_____

_____

2. If you could go on a space trip for free, would you take it? Why or why not? State your reasons.

_____

_____

_____

_____

_____

### Word Bank

| | |
|---|---|
| 1. the Big Bang (n.) (宇宙起源) 大爆炸 | 7. extraordinary (adj.) 令人驚奇的 |
| 2. frontiers (n. pl) 極限 | 8. gravity (n.) 地球引力 |
| 3. awe (n.) 驚嘆 | 9. infinite (adj.) 無限的；極大的 |
| 4. dimension (n.) 維 (構成空間的因素) | 10. bizarre (adj.) 異乎尋常的 |
| 5. astronomy (n.) 天文學 | 11. complexity (n.) 複雜性 |
| 6. revolutionary (adj.) 革命性的；創新的 | 12. contemplate (v.) 思量；預期 |

It is a well-known fact that the planet's oceans are becoming increasingly polluted. Oil and other chemicals in the ocean are having a devastating impact on life depending on oceans. Another less well-known source of pollution is plastic.

According to the latest research, our oceans are being besieged by large quantities of plastic. In the Pacific Ocean, an estimated 705,000 tons of trash has collected in two large areas; one off the coast of Japan and the other near California. Together they are known as the Great Pacific Garbage Patch. Much of that floating trash is plastic, which breaks down into smaller pieces over time, but it never goes away. Unfortunately, seabirds often eat pieces of plastic, mistaking it for food.

Scientists have been analyzing the amount of plastic that seabirds consume since the 1960s. Only 5% of seabirds had plastic in their stomach in the sixties, but that figure had jumped to 80% in the eighties and today it stands at 90%. These data **do not bode well** for the future of our oceans and the creatures that live in them. The abundance of plastic found in seabirds should serve as a warning. But what can be done to tackle the plastic crisis in our oceans?

One of the most promising ideas is a recent invention called the Seabin. The device automatically filters seawater and removes oil, fuel, chemicals, and floating trash, such as plastic bottles. The Seabin can be placed in harbors, rivers, lakes, and so on. However, it is important to remember that technology alone will not solve this major environmental issue. Governments around the world must work together to combat the problem of ocean plastic. If we don't take action today, seabirds could one day become a distant memory.

下列四題請依據文章之文意選出最適當的一個選項。

_____ 1. What is the purpose of this passage?　　　此題判斷 _____

　　(A) To fill the gaps in our knowledge of Pacific seabirds.

　　(B) To emphasize the importance of seabird conservation.

　　(C) To impose a ban on the purchase of plastic products.

　　(D) To arouse global concern about ocean plastic pollution.

_____ 2. According to the passage, all of the following are　　此題判斷 _____
　　threats to marine animals EXCEPT _____.

　　(A) oil spill　　　　　　　　　(B) floating driftwood

　　(C) plastic trash　　　　　　　(D) chemical waste

_____ 3. Which of the following statements is true?　　此題判斷 _____

　　(A) The Great Pacific Garbage Patch is formed by the trash collected along the
　　　coasts of only one country.

　　(B) As time passes by, plastic trash will break down into very tiny particles and
　　　then totally disappear.

　　(C) Nowadays, the percentage of seabird plastic consumption is eighteen times
　　　the number of that in the 1960s.

　　(D) The Seabin is an outdated invention because it can only remove solid waste
　　　like plastic bottles.

_____ 4. What does the phrase "**do not bode well**" in the　　此題判斷 _____
　　third paragraph mean?

　　(A) There are no feasible solutions to the grave ocean plastic crisis.

　　(B) More and more seabirds will be exposed to plastic waste and eat it.

　　(C) The Seabin project won't work well enough to tackle plastic trash.

　　(D) Technology alone will not solve the thorny environmental issue.

閱讀完文章後，請針對下列問題用英文表達自己的想法與觀點。

1. Now the ocean plastic pollution is getting worse and worse. As a member of the global village, what can we do to reduce ocean plastic waste in our daily life? Provide some possible solutions.

_____

_____

_____

2. Look at the picture below. Guess what happened to the seabird before, and then describe its current condition. Last, what do you think will happen next in the future?

_____

_____

_____

## Word Bank

| | |
|---|---|
| 1. devastating (adj.) 破壞性的；毀滅性的 | 6. abundance (n.) 大量 |
| 2. besiege (v.) 圍住；包圍 | 7. tackle (v.) 處理 |
| 3. the Great Pacific Garbage Patch (n.) 太平洋垃圾帶 | 8. the Seabin (n.) 海洋垃圾桶裝置 |
| 4. break down (v.) 分解 | 9. filter (v.) 過濾 |
| 5. bode (v.) 預示；是⋯的兆頭 | 10. combat (v.) 對付；與⋯戰鬥 |

The Darwin Awards is a not-so-serious honor given to those who have died from their own stupidity and therefore have contributed to mankind by removing themselves from the gene-pool.

The name for the Darwin Awards comes from Charles Darwin who formulated the theory of evolution by natural selection. Natural selection is the theory that species change or improve over time as animals with inadequate genes die before they can reproduce. In the case of the Darwin Awards, the inadequate genes are stupidity.

The Darwin Awards originates from the early days of the Internet. The first references to the awards were in 1985 with posts describing the awards as being given after death to those "who keep their genes out of our pool." Not just anyone who dies from their own stupidity can receive an award. It has to be from interesting or funny circumstances as well. For example, the terrorist who sent a letter bomb in 2000. The letter didn't have enough postage stamps and was sent back to him. He opened the letter without realizing it was his own bomb and died.

To be awarded a Darwin Award, you must be unable to reproduce, so you have to be either dead or **sterile**. Nominees must have died or become sterile from their own extremely poor judgment. They also need to be capable of making responsible decisions, i.e. they must be an adult and not suffer from mental defects. Finally, the source of the story has to be reliable, such as from newspapers and television reports.

Some notable awards include when James Burns attempted to fix a truck while his friend was driving it. He was underneath it when his shirt caught on something and was found "wrapped around the drive shaft." Another was when someone in Michigan decided to move a downed electric cable from his car with his hands and died from electrocution. One man tried to jump off a 70 feet bridge with a 70 feet bungee cord, forgetting that bungee cords stretch.

As you can see, while these awards are definitely tragic, it's difficult not to laugh at the ridiculous ways these people have died.

下列四題請依據文章之文意選出最適當的一個選項。

_____ 1. What is the best title for this passage?　此題判斷 _____

(A) Natural Selection: The Theory Behind the Darwin Awards.

(B) Stupidity: What Keeps Inadequate Genes out of Human's Pool.

(C) The Darwin Awards: Dying Has Never Been So Funny.

(D) Die a Fun Death: Incredible Stories You Should Know.

_____ 2. Which of the following statements about the Darwin Awards is NOT true?　此題判斷 _____

(A) It is named after the founder of an evolutionary theory.

(B) The first online appearance of the award was in 1985.

(C) Foolishness is the deficient genes it wants to remove.

(D) It is awarded exclusively to those who are already dead.

_____ 3. According to the passage, a potential candidate for the Darwin Awards should meet all of the following requirements EXCEPT _____.　此題判斷 _____

(A) inability to reproduce

(B) age limit

(C) foolish death caused by others

(D) stupid judgment

_____ 4. Which of the following is closest in meaning to "**sterile**" in the fourth paragraph?　此題判斷 _____

(A) Infertile.　　　　　　(B) Mortal.

(C) Energetic.　　　　　　(D) Serious.

閱讀完文章後，請針對下列問題用英文表達自己的想法與觀點。

1.What do you think about the Darwin Awards? Express your ideas.

_____

_____

_____

_____

2.What is the stupidest thing you have ever done? Describe it.

_____

_____

_____

_____

## Word Bank

| | |
|---|---|
| 1. stupidity (n.) 愚蠢；蠢行 | 8. notable (adj.) 值得注意的；顯要的 |
| 2. gene pool (n.) 基因庫 | 9. underneath (prep.) 在…底下 |
| 3. formulate (v.) 想出；規劃 | 10. catch on (v.) 勾住 |
| 4. natural selection (n.) 天擇；自然選擇 | 11. drive shaft (n.) 汽車的驅動軸 |
| 5. postage (n.) 郵資；郵費 | 12. downed (adj.) 落下的；被擊落的 |
| 6. sterile (adj.) 不孕的；無法生育的 | 13. electrocution (n.) 觸電身亡 |
| 7. nominee (n.) 被提名者 | 14. bungee cord (n.) 彈力繩 |

## Answer Key

| Unit | 1. | 2. | 3. | 4. |
|------|-----|-----|-----|-----|
| 1 | (B), main idea | (D), main idea | (A), main idea | (B), writer's attitude |
| 2 | (C), supporting details | (B), supporting details | (D), words in context | (C), words in context |
| 3 | (B), reference | (C), inference | (D), inference | (C), prediction |
| 4 | (B), main idea | (C), supporting details | (D), words in context | (C), inference |
| 5 | (B), supporting details | (C), main idea | (D), words in context | (C), prediction |
| 6 | (C), main idea | (D), reference | (A), supporting details | (B), inference |
| 7 | (C), main idea | (B), supporting details | (D), supporting details | (D), words in context |
| 8 | (D), supporting details | (A), supporting details | (C), main idea | (A), words in context |
| 9 | (C), supporting details | (C), main idea | (D), words in context | (D), supporting details |
| 10 | (B), main idea | (C), supporting details | (D), words in context | (A), supporting details |
| 11 | (C), main idea | (B), supporting details | (D), supporting details | (B), inference |
| 12 | (B), main idea | (C), supporting details | (D), inference | (C), writer's tone |
| 13 | (D), main idea | (C), words in context | (A), supporting details | (B), writer's attitude |
| 14 | (B), supporting details | (D), reference | (C), supporting details | (C), inference |
| 15 | (D), main idea | (B), supporting details | (C), supporting details | (B), words in context |
| 16 | (C), main idea | (D), supporting details | (C), supporting details | (A), words in context |

# 哈佛英聽講堂

★ 學校團訂送三回完全仿照大考聽力測驗的贈卷

曾郁淇／著

修煉60堂英語聽講課，讓頂尖大學都想錄取你。
跟著哈佛學生一起學，聽說英文超簡單！

- 結合會話與聽力練習，同步提昇聽、說兩項能力。
- 題型仿照大考英聽及新多益題目，兩種考試一本搞定。
- 附贈完整聽力題目腳本及中譯。
- 全書特聘專業外籍錄音員錄製，母語人士口音一聽就懂。
- 題型多元，包含照片、圖表、海報、機上廣播等生活化情境，不只準備考試，更能強化日常生活必備的英語力。

# 大考英文搖分樹

黃淑媛、林依依、洪珮菱／編著

考前十四週衝刺，
一本《搖分樹》讓你大考搖高分！
本書嚴選學測範圍內重要的單字、片語、文法、句型，依冊次分成共十四回，每回皆有試題測驗，幫助學生考前十四週做最後衝刺。

# 英文這樣寫，不NG

張淑娸、應惠蕙／編著　車蓓群／審定

Write Right！讓所有文章都不NG！

- 由「句子擴充」、「內容構思」的概念談起，引導您從最基礎的寫作開始。
- 提點常見的寫作錯誤，如標點符號、時態等，替您打下紮實的基本功。
- 介紹常見文體，包括記敘文、描寫文、論說文、應用文等，讓您充分學習。
- 補充自傳、讀書計畫等寫作技巧，幫助您為生涯規劃加分。
- 循序漸進引導，按部就班練習，自學、教學都不NG！

*Intermediate*

★ 全民英檢初／中級適用
★ 學科能力測驗／指定科目考試／統一入學測驗適用

# 英文讀寫 萬試通

解析本

政治大學外文中心副教授
車蓓群　審定
三民英語編輯小組　彙編

三民書局

# Contents

**Unit 1**    1

**Unit 2**    2

**Unit 3**    3

**Unit 4**    4

**Unit 5**    5

**Unit 6**    6

**Unit 7**    7

**Unit 8**    8

**Unit 9**    9

**Unit 10**    10

**Unit 11**    11

**Unit 12**    12

**Unit 13**    13

**Unit 14**    14

**Unit 15**    15

**Unit 16**    16

## 實戰演練

　　由鴨或鵝的肝臟製成的肝醬是一道有爭議的佳餚，其豐富口感與奶油質地備受推崇。鵝肝醬的爭議來自強迫灌食的製造方法，讓一些人認為殘忍、不人道。

　　鳥禽增胖的方法自古流傳而來。羅馬時代首次提到鵝肝醬，古羅馬人藉著餵食鵝隻無花果來撐大牠們的肝臟。羅馬帝國衰亡後，直到猶太族群再次發現用來烹煮油脂的增胖鵝隻有口感豐富鮮美的增大肝臟，鵝肝醬才再度成為歐洲佳餚。

　　傳統肝醬由鵝製成，但現今 95% 的肝醬由鴨的肝臟製成。準備邊徙時，一些鳥類擴大喉嚨吞進整條魚以備之後消化。如此一來自然增肥、撐大了牠們的肝臟。鵝鴨先以為期 90 天逐漸增加餵食的方式增胖，之後再以胃管灌食玉米 12 至 15 天。胃管灌食是一個漏斗連接一根管子深入到鵝鴨擴大的喉嚨強迫灌食。餵以油脂烹煮的食用玉米來增肥肝臟、製造奶油口感。法國是目前鵝肝醬最大的生產與消費國。鵝肝醬多被認為是奢侈品，通常在特殊場合才食用。

　　一些人認為胃管灌食鵝鴨殘忍、不人道，歐洲許多國家因此禁止此方法生產的肝製品。遭到強迫灌食的鵝鴨不但面對餵食者產生恐懼並壓力倍增。雖然正常狀況下鴨或鵝的肝臟能增大 50%，但作為鵝肝醬用途的肝臟尺寸卻增大為原本的 10 倍。

　　鵝鴨用來製作肝醬的飼養方式仍持續爭論。最終，讓這些動物為了成就一件奢侈品而承受如此苦難是否值得？值得深思。

1. 答案為：(B)。此題判斷為 main idea。略讀後找出第一句 Foie gras is a controversial delicacy made from the liver of a duck or goose 即為主題句，後面兩句支持句分別說明鵝肝醬的美味及強迫灌食之殘忍，故選(B)。選項(C)只提到強迫灌食為不人道的折磨，未提及「主題 Foie gras」，故不可選。

2. 答案為：(D)。此題判斷為 main idea。本題無法只靠找出主題句，來判斷本文的目的。所以可快速略讀每段首尾兩句。而從第一段和第四段可拼湊出重複的關鍵資訊 controversial、force-feeding、cruel、inhumane，由此可知此為作者強調之處及其寫作目的所在，故選(D)。

3. 答案為：(A)。此題判斷為 main idea。略讀後找出第二段第一句 The method of fattening birds has been known and used since ancient times 即為主題句，後面陳述的事實發展作為支持句，可知本段描述鵝肝醬發展的歷史，故選(A)。

4. 答案為：(B)。此題判斷為 writer's attitude。略讀後可發現作者從第一段就指出鵝肝醬之爭議以及不人道的強迫灌食方式，全文除第一段一句話介紹鵝肝醬的美味外，其他地方未多加讚揚。再加上最後一句用問句反詰：Ultimately, is it worth subjecting these animals to such an ordeal for what amounts to a luxury?，可知作者「不贊同」為了美食犧牲動物權利的態度，故選(B)。選項(C) Pessimistic 為誘答項，雖然它是負面形容詞，但作者在文章中「積極」地提供了許多有關鵝肝醬製程及相關事實，態度「並不消極」，故不可選。

## 回答問題

1. My favorite foreign food is Italian pizza, which is made of flat dough with different toppings. I like it because it comes in a variety of flavors, such as seafood, beef, pork, cheese, and so on. With so many delicious and colorful toppings on the pizza, it looks like a beautiful palette of colors and always gives me a good appetite. The second reason is that eating pizza is a fun activity for me to enjoy with my family and friends. We can share the pizza together, eating, chatting, and strengthening our relationship. Eating pizza can always put me in a happy mood, and that's why I like it so much.

2. Though foie gras is considered a delicacy and a luxury by some people, I am still against the production and selling of it for the following reasons. First, we should not base our enjoyment of delicacies on other animals' suffering. We should respect lives, including those of animals. Animals have the right to live free of suffering like humans. Second, there are other foods more delicious and healthier to our bodies than foie gras. We don't need to make ducks or geese suffer just to satisfy our taste buds. I believe that people can only stay healthy by eating "happy" food rather than "painful" food.

## 實戰演練

是什麼讓你害怕?你認為自己能將這種恐懼投入到拍攝恐怖片嗎?如果你認為這很容易,再想想。

拍攝恐怖片是一件非常困難的工作,導演必須熟知真正嚇人的元素,他們在拍攝恐怖片時也必須善用恐懼心理學。A. D. Calvo 在《電影人雜誌》寫道,一部優秀的恐怖片涵蓋許多不同層面,理解是什麼讓人們害怕總是重要,它必須用適當的氛圍呈現。他稱之為「陰沉的視覺暗示」:帶出觀眾普遍的恐懼感。除此之外,一定要有懸疑感。如果你預料到即將發生的事,如何能感到驚訝?讓觀眾渾然不知後續發展是引發尖叫最佳的方式。

Calvo 也提到不同的拍攝構圖技巧,例如透過樹枝或從窗簾後方拍攝。當以這種角度看,可以幫助提供觀眾片中不祥力量的觀點。這幫助觀眾知道有人或東西正監視著。 這些技巧也幫助營造毛骨悚然的情緒,正如同燈光、音效甚至電影配樂的功效。

許多恐怖片中的一個重要部分是突如其來的驚嚇。這是螢幕發生的事突然嚇到你,讓你真的從椅子上跳起。突如其來的驚嚇可以是真實的,例如當一頭恐怖的怪獸突然出現;或者可以是「虛假」的。一個「虛假的」突如其來的驚嚇發生在雖然與故事無關,但觀眾仍感到驚訝的時候。突然的聲響,舉例來說,房裡有隻貓撞倒花瓶、讓花瓶粉碎在地,就製造一個「虛假的」突如其來的驚嚇。

最後,拍攝恐怖片涵蓋許多,不是一個容易駕馭的類型。然而如果你使用一些試驗過的技巧,你或許能以恐怖片製片者之姿獲得成功。

1. 答案為:(C)。此題判斷為 supporting details。掃讀後將題目中 "NOT a necessary aspect" 圈出來 ,然後在文章第二段第 4 行找到相對應的 "aspects",可知本題詢問第二段的細節。接著再用掃讀在第 3 行圈出與選項(A)對應的 "the psychology of fear"、第 5 行的 "a proper atmosphere",及第 7 行的 "suspense",可知(A)(B)(D)皆為製作恐怖片的要素,(C)選項並未提及。

2. 答案為:(B)。此題判斷為 supporting details。掃讀後將題目中 "framing techniques" 圈出來 ,然後在文章第三段第 1 行找到對應的相同詞彙,可知本題詢問第三~四段的細節。在第三段最後一句可圈出與選項(B)對應的 "lighting, sound effects and the film score",故(B)為正解。

3. 答案為:(D)。此題判斷為 words in context。掃讀後,在第 2 段第 7 行找到對應的目標單字。接著利用上下文線索,掃讀圈出後面兩句的關鍵字 "If you know what is going to happen next, why would you be surprised?" (作者 「舉例」 說明 suspense),及 "keeping the audience in the dark" (作者用同義片語來「重述解釋」suspense),可知 suspense 就是將觀眾蒙在鼓裡,「延遲告訴」他們後續發展,故選(D)。

4. 答案為:(C)。此題判斷為 words in context。掃讀後將題目中 "sinister" 圈出來,然後在文章第三段第 3 行找到對應的目標單字。 接著利用上下文線索 , 掃讀圈出後面兩句的關鍵字 "someone or something is watching" 及 "a creepy mood" (作者「舉例」解釋 sinister 的感覺),可知 sinister 是一種負面的感覺,故選(C) Evil。

## 回答問題

1. I like to watch horror films for the following reasons. First, watching horror films is a good way for me to relieve stress by screaming out loud. They can evoke my fear and allow me to experience fear in a safe environment. Second, watching horror films is a social event with friends or family for me. I can accomplish something dreadful and overcome my fear with others and thus foster our relationship while watching films. That's why I like horror films.

2. I will choose to watch "The Incredible Journey" because I like animal stories, and I also keep two pet dogs in my house. Another reason is that the film title caught my eye by implying that there must be something fun and touching during the trip. As to the storyline of the film, I think it is about four stray animals, a rooster, a cat, a dog and a donkey, who go on an incredible journey. They strive to find a safe place to settle down. Despite the difficulties and challenges they face, they will work together and deal with all the crises. I think the four animals will eventually reach their goal and live happily together.

# Unit 3

## ⏱ 實戰演練

　　法律訂定最低工資乍看能自動讓社會中較貧困的成員受惠，讓他們更富裕，保證他們有足夠的收入過生活。因此他們能使用這筆錢購買國內企業製造的產品以提振國家經濟。他們的所得稅也幫助政府支付醫療與教育等的服務。

　　另一方面，一些經濟學家認為事情並不如此單純。他們聲稱工資條例干預自然經濟的運作，因為勞力本身是資本社會中市場的一部分。因此如果資本主義要有效運作的話，勞工的工資應該像價格一般反映供需法則。

　　例如，如果景氣好，企業會招募更多員工並支付更高的薪水；如果經濟不佳，公司會減薪以續營。當經濟不景氣時，基本工資會阻擋雇主徵聘新人，因為勞工過於昂貴。這會導致許多勞工失業、沒有收入。此外，這也可能鼓勵小型企業以低薪聘僱非法勞工。因為這些勞工沒有繳稅，以致社會將不能受惠。

　　然而，從另一個角度來看，這是個侷限的分析：薪資視同只是另一個價格而無視問題中的人性。最低工資應與勞工安全一般考量，也就是說，這是個社會議題，而非僅僅是經濟議題。若以這種態度，一個合適的解決辦法便是設立最低工資，但不能過低或過高，勞資雙方才能互利。

1. 答案為：Ⓑ。此題判斷為 reference。掃讀後找出指涉題 this 位於第三段第 4 行，接著利用上下文線索，判斷 this 在此代替前面一個句子「最低工資讓老闆在經濟蕭條時不想雇用員工，因為工資太高」，故選擇答案Ⓑ。之後再將Ⓑ「經濟蕭條工資昂貴」代入第 4 行句子，可再次確認此答案正確。選項Ⓐ文章未提，故不可選。選項Ⓒ為誘答項，雖然「雇用低薪非法勞工」也會讓很多人因此失業，但是指涉詞 this 必須代替「前面」出現過的名詞或句子，選項Ⓒ是 this「後面」的內容，故不可選。選項Ⓓ文章未提，故不可選。

2. 答案為：Ⓒ。此題判斷為 inference。因為掃讀後可找出本句在第二段第 1 行的位置，利用上下文線索和思考後，可發現本句旨在針對第一段「最低工資可幫助弱勢勞工，並讓政府有財源推行醫療及教育等社會福利」，提出反駁。接著在本句後面便舉例說明「最低工資如何干預自由經濟中的供需原理」。因此，談論最低工資時，除了勞方和政府的利益外，其實也應該考量資方的利益，故

選擇Ⓒ。

3. 答案為：Ⓓ。此題判斷為 inference。略讀文章後，再利用掃讀圈出作者在第四段裡，敘述最低工資的關鍵字：employees' safety、a social issue、not merely an economic one (issue)。接著再運用思考能力，即能推論作者隱含的意思為：只將最低工資看成經濟議題，而忽略勞工安全，將讓最低工資變成社會議題。由此可推知若無最低工資保障勞工，當勞工生活出現困難，就可能導致這種社會問題，故選Ⓓ。

4. 答案為：Ⓒ。此題判斷為 prediction。預測型題目通常必須從文章最後幾行，推測接下來可能的發展。本文最後一句提及「最低工資解決的折衷辦法，就是能夠設定讓勞資雙方都受益、不會太高或太低的最低工資」，由此可預測接下來可能會介紹「如何設定讓雙方都能受益的最低工資」，故選擇Ⓒ。

## ✎ 回答問題

1. Yes, I think I will definitely apply for the job. As a tourist ambassador, I will have the chance to explore the tropical island and enjoy beautiful ocean views while patrolling the beaches. Besides fulfilling my job duties by sharing the beauty of the island via social media, I can take advantage of my stay there to sail, scuba dive, or even swim with fish in the beautiful ocean. In a word, I think this job is like a paid holiday.

2. I approve minimum wages and my reasons are as follows. First, it is governments' duty to protect low-skilled workers against exploitation. Therefore, governments should stand with underprivileged workers rather than with big businesses, and minimum wages should be adjusted frequently so as to combat inflation. Second, we should not view workers as a price or an object. I believe that only when disadvantaged workers lead a stable life can our society remain stable and our economy keep booming.

## 🕐 實戰演練

　　嬰兒是小科學家，他們的大腦結構與成人的截然不同。這些年幼孩童能夠比我們原先認為的學習更多，並改變以往我們對早期學習的認知，這是過去幾年密集研究早期童年，加州大學柏克萊分校心理學家艾莉森·高普尼克得到的結論。

　　「相較於成人，嬰兒建立更多神經連結與突觸」，高普尼克說道，「所以彷彿在初期，我們有這個全為學習而設計的大腦——非常靈活、可塑，大量回應各種經驗。之後當我們長大，有顆更像是一台精實出色機器的大腦，完全為了辦好事情而設計，但就不夠靈活、不夠擅長學習新事物」。

　　當年幼孩童玩玩具，他們貌似科學家做實驗，透過主動觀察、探索、想像與實驗來學習這個世界的運作方式。但許多人將「學習」等同於傳統在學校教育年長孩子的教學方式，他們聲稱孩子應該由父母或師長教導如何學習。然而針對年幼孩童玩耍的研究指出：如果「教導」孩子用特定方式玩玩具，他們會模仿這個行為而不自己實驗，最後學習到的反而比較少。

　　根據她的實驗，高普尼克主張我們不需要教導孩子如何學習，嬰兒與年幼孩童天生好奇、愛探索，我們只需關愛、照顧他們，並給他們不受干擾、自由玩耍的機會——學習自然應運而生。

1. 答案為：(B)。此題判斷為 main idea。略讀後找出第一句 Babies are little scientists ... 即為主題句，後面的支持句說明幼童能夠學習的事物，遠超過我們想像。後面各段內容進一步闡述幼童具有主動觀察、探究、想像及實驗等能力，可確認本文主旨為「幼童是天生的學習者」，故選(B)。誘答項(D)雖與早期學習有關，但早期學習的目的並非讓嬰幼兒成為心理學家，故不可選。

2. 答案為：(C)。此題判斷為 supporting details。掃讀後圈出題目的關鍵字"babies"、"NOT excel"及"adults"，可知此題旨在比較嬰兒遜於成人之處，在第二段可找到相對應的細節內容。掃讀後圈出(C)選項的"machine"，在第5行可找到對應內容，可知像機器般精準完美完成任務的能力，是成人勝過嬰兒，故(C)為本題答案。

3. 答案為：(D)。此題判斷為 words in context。掃讀後，在第四段最後一行找到對應的目標單字。接著利用上下文線索，掃讀圈出第一句的關鍵字

"we don't have to teach young children how to learn"，及最後一句的關鍵字"learning will naturally follow"，由此可知作者暗示我們根本不必教幼童如何學習，他們自然而然就會學習，可推知本句中 interference 所指的，就是父母師長的教導，故選(D)。

4. 答案為：(C)。此題判斷為 inference。本題須了解文章大意為「嬰幼兒天生即具學習天賦，父母師長不必教導他們如何學習」。因此，作者於下一段所舉的例證，必須符合此教育理念，故(C)為正確答案。

## ✏️ 回答問題

1. Yes, though we may not be as creative and plastic as babies, we can still learn new things by observing and exploring them. I consider it feasible to "flip" our learning if given more flexible learning periods to do so. That is, our teachers can just give us materials (toys) and then let us read (play with) them ourselves. After that, we can share what we learn and discuss with others. Therefore, I really think the method can be applied to us, and I can learn better this way.

2. Yes, I agree that we will have a higher retention rate by teaching others. As a proverb goes, "He who teaches learns." If I want to teach others something, I need to have a full understanding of what I am teaching. Besides, during the teaching process, the repetition and practice involved will also increase my retention rate. For example, I once surfed the Internet to understand the usage of an English grammar rule before I explained it to my classmate. After that, both my classmate and I benefited a lot and I really remembered things better!

## 實戰演練

十九世紀工業革命帶來巨變，手工製造的產品改以機器自動化生產。產品更快、更便宜的製造，但生產力提升帶來新問題，許多低技術勞工失業。同樣情形也發生於電腦問世後自動化生產加速的時代。

但仍有許多工作是機械絕不能勝任，是吧？請再想想。現在日本已有機器人取代客服，例如長崎豪斯登堡機器人酒店，其職員全是機器人。這些機器人造型像人類，四肢可移動並能變換臉部表情。他們能夠招呼客人、用多種語言回答問題，甚至預約計程車。它們雖然仍無法與人們流暢溝通，但已快速變得更世故，誰知道緊接而來是什麼？

這是另一個科技改變時代的開端嗎？有待觀察。這些機器人貌似人類，但無法像我們一樣思考。真正的機器人需要人工智慧，但這距離全面實現仍有一段差距。

這並未阻擋人類思索一個透過機器人全面自動化的社會會是何種模樣。一些人認為這將會淘汰多數的非專業人士，因他們無法提供價值給權貴人士。如果不需在工廠工作、沖咖啡或駕駛計程車，大部分的人將如何謀生？工業與資訊時代皆引發相同的預測，但這樣的新科技相較於奪走，實際上卻創造更多工作機會；並且因產能增加，人們的生活水平也得到提升。

1. 答案為：(B)。此題判斷為 <u>supporting details</u>。掃讀後圈出題目關鍵字 "changes" 及 "the Industrial Revolution"，然後可在第一段找到對應內容：「工業革命帶來的改變」。選項(A)自動化 (第2行)、選項(C)生產力 (第3行)、以及選項(D)失業問題 (第4行)；選項(B)醫療保健服務並未包含在內，為本題答案。

2. 答案為：(C)。此題判斷為 <u>main idea</u>。本題除了找出第二段的大意外，還要進一步從第二句的 "Think again." ，推敲出作者真正的意思，其實是「反駁」第一句 "Still, there are many jobs a machine could never do"。因此，作者在第二段提及機器人的目的，即是告知讀者「機器人的出現，會大大改變未來就業市場的結構」，後面並舉例說明這個不可避免的趨勢：日本尖端先進的機器人除了對話能力外，其他方面幾乎和人類差不多，因此選項(C)為正解。其他選項為第二段舉例的內容，並非在本段提及機器人的目的，故皆不可選。

3. 答案為：(D)。此題判斷為 words in context。掃讀後，在第二段第 6 行可找到對應的目標單字。接著利用上下文線索，可發現作者在前幾行「舉例」說明目前機器人的功能及外型已十分先進，未來會變得更加 "sophisticated"，由此推知它們應該會變得更加「先進與複雜」，故選(D)。

4. 答案為：(C)。此題判斷為 prediction。預測型題目通常必須從文章最後幾行，推測接下來可能的發展。最後一段提到工業和資訊時代都預測非專業工作將被機器人取代，但最後一句提到：這項新科技「實際上所創造出來的工作機會，比被它所取代的更多」，由此可預測接下來可能會介紹「機器人時代的工作機會」，故選擇(C)。

## 回答問題

1. Yes, I would like to stay in a hotel run by robots because it will be a novel experience. I imagine in such a hotel, a robotic concierge will first greet me in Chinese and help me check in. It will also explain breakfast times and locations. After that, I will go into my room and find my personal hotel butler, a cute little robot in it. It will switch on the lights, offer weather forecasts and take care of all my requests throughout my stay at the hotel. I think the fun and comfort I experience at the robot-staffed hotel will absolutely enrich my travel memories.

2. With the advance of new technology, some low-skilled or repetitive jobs may be replaced by robots for the sake of increasing efficiency, such as customer service representatives, salespeople, hotel and bank receptionists, museum tour guides, drivers, etc. However, robots are created by people, so industry associated with designing, caring for, and even recycling the mechanical and electronic parts of robots will emerge. In addition, people have great creativity that robots lack for; therefore, jobs like art, fashion, or landscape designers, writers, singers, musicians, and choreographers won't be taken over by robots.

## 🕐 實戰演練

網路直播是指經由網路播放多媒體，最初設計作為娛樂用途。第一個網路直播由蘋果公司於1995年推出，它在紐約夜店播送演唱會聲音。之後，標準音頻加上影像的網路直播快速發展，搖滾樂團得以使用來現場網路直播演唱會。

自此之後，網路直播成為全球現象。相較於傳統電視使用衛星播送，專業的網路直播價格更低廉，因此人們能負擔在婚禮等大事的網路直播費用。今日一般人能利用免費科技在家網路直播。舉例來說在韓國，一位迷人的女士透過網路直播自己吃飯，快速竄紅，在她吃飯同時，也與觀眾閒聊，藉由影迷的贊助謀生。

網路直播也成為主要的商業特色，企業利用網路直播會議與教育訓練的影片給全球雇員觀看。其他人利用這項科技進行行銷、銷售。此外，網路直播也大幅度影響教學。許多專業機構會宣傳特定主題的網路直播，而觀眾付費觀賞專家學者提供的網路直播。大學講課使用網路直播，這在數百萬人修習的線上課程尤其普遍。

人們往往認為網路直播受限於即時發生事件的現象。然而雖然網路直播多單純是現場轉播的生活事件，但其中許多已錄製存檔。全球最大的美國國會圖書館就存有不同主題、數以千計的網路直播。因此網路直播很可能在儲存人類知識上對未來世代有重要貢獻。

1. 答案為：(C)。此題判斷為 main idea。本題詢問倒數第二段 (即第三段) 的大意。略讀後找出第一句 "Webcasting has also become a major feature of business" 即為本段主題句，後面列舉一般公司如何利用網路直播進行線上會議、員工訓練、行銷，以及其他教育訓練機構和大學，也會利用網路直播提供線上課程，尤其可知本段大意為「不同行業如何運用網路直播技術，並從中獲益」，故選項(C)為正確答案。

2. 答案為：(D)。此題判斷為 reference。掃讀後找出指涉題 these 位於第三段第6行，接著利用上下文線索，判斷 these 在此代替前面的複數名詞「直播節目 webcasts」，故選擇答案(D)。之後再將(D)的 webcasts 代入第6行句子，可再次確認此答案正確。

3. 答案為：(A)。此題判斷為 supporting details。掃

讀後圈出選項(A)的關鍵字 "first audio plus video webcast"、"Apple" 和 "1995"，然後可在第一段第2～3行找到對應內容，但蘋果公司最早僅能進行「聲音」直播，沒有「影像」部分，故選項(A)錯誤，為本題答案。

4. 答案為：(B)。此題判斷為 inference。本題測試讀者是否能在略讀全文之後，利用作者提供的暗示性訊息，拼湊上下文線索，再利用掃讀圈出作者用來敘述網路直播的關鍵字，推論出目前網路直播比起其他媒體形式，更受到大眾青睞的特質：更具娛樂效果 (entertainment，第一段第2行)、現場或非現場直播 (live/real time; recorded/saved，第一段第4行、第四段第1～3行)、較便宜 (much cheaper，第二段第2行)、免費直播軟體 (free technology，第二段第4行)，綜合以上特點，可推論目前網路直播比起其他媒體形式，對大眾「更具吸引力」，故選擇(B)。

## ✏️ 回答問題

1. Yes, I have watched karaoke webcasts in my free time. The broadcasters are a couple who sing, tell funny jokes and chat with viewers. Sometimes viewers can also sing karaoke with the broadcasters and interact with each other. Though the quality of the webcasts may leave much to be desired, the real-time interaction, variety, fun and novel elements, mobility, and low costs still attract a lot of viewers' attention. I think webcasts can bring joy to our lives, but we should also choose carefully and control the time spent on them.

2. No, I won't. I think I will have higher motivation learning at school than watching webcast courses. I like to interact with my teachers and classmates face to face. The greatest value of classroom instruction lies in its human touch, and this is what online webcast courses can't provide. Therefore, I won't take them as the main learning method (maybe OK as a supplementary one), and I think they are more suitable for people who have good self-discipline and need a flexible learning style.

## 🕐 實戰演練

對觀察潮汐的人來說，海水在低潮時看似向後拉、在高潮時隨著水平線向前推。

事實上，這股引力是垂直的。月球由上施加引力使正下方的海水實際向上拉而鼓起，這形成了月球正下方地區的高潮。一些人推論得出，地球相對側的海水也應該同等程度地上升，因此形成該側的低潮。然而，這是一個錯誤的推測。月球引力將地球拉向月球的同時，也吸引潮汐隆起之中與周圍的海水。月球引力在地球相對兩側的影響最小，所以地球兩側的海水移動最少，形成潮汐隆起、創造另一個漲潮，因此在月亮與地球垂直線的兩端形成低潮。

地球每日繞地軸自轉一周形成一天兩次漲退潮。一地區的低潮發生在地球遠離月亮的正下方，約十二小時後該地區再次繞回月球之下時恢復高潮，但這兩者間存在地球的質量。十二小時後此地區會再次停留在月球正下方，這時兩者間只有大氣存在。

潮汐對我們的祖先來說很重要。漁夫發現退潮時魚群大量聚集，這讓他們在退潮時能更有效率地捕魚。此外，潮汐在人類的未來很可能扮演重大角色：它們可以作為乾淨可再生能源的主要來源。潮汐發電站運用潮汐作用轉動渦輪，將水力轉變為電力。

1. 答案為：(C)。此題判斷為 main idea。本題無法只靠找出主題句來判斷文章大意，因此須快速略讀每段首尾兩句，來拼湊資訊。之後由第二段的首句 "In fact, the pull is vertical" 及第三段的首句 "The earth rotating on its axis once a day causes the phenomenon of two daily tides"，可知本文前三段在介紹潮汐如何形成。另外，由第四段的首句 " Tides were important to our ancestors" 可推知潮汐對地球的重要性。由二～四段主題句，便可拼湊出本文主要在於 "To introduce tides and their importance to earth"，故選(C)。

2. 答案為：(B)。此題判斷為 supporting details。另外，學生必須將第二段描述漲潮形成的細節文字，轉譯成圖像。掃讀後將題目中 "high tides" 及 "second paragraph" 圈出來，然後到文章第二段尋找相對應的內容。接著再用掃讀在第 3 行圈出 "high tides in regions directly below the moon"、第 7 行的 "the earth's opposite end, so the water there remains and forms a bulge, creating another high tide"、及第 8 行的 "Low tides

therefore form at the sides of the vertical line of moon and earth"，可知漲潮形成的地點是「正對著月球的下方」及「背對月球同一地點處」；而退潮形成於月球與地球垂直線的兩端，故選(B)。

3. 答案為：(D)。此題判斷為 supporting details。掃讀後選項(D)在第四段第 1～2 行找到對應內容，可知退潮 (ebb) 時魚群聚集，為捕魚最佳時機，故(D)選項正確。

4. 答案為：(D)。此題判斷為 words in context。掃讀後，在第 2 段第 2 行找到對應的目標單字。接著利用上下文線索，掃讀圈出前句中的線索 "dragged upward" 及後面一句對於 bulge 所作的解釋 "This forms the high tides"，故選(D)。

## ✏️ 回答問題

1. My favorite proverb is the second one, "Take charge of your life! The tides do not command the ship. The sailor does." I like it because it sheds light on the importance of taking charge of our own lives rather than giving in to the obstacles we encounter in life. Furthermore, it carries a positive meaning and serves as a reminder that I should always be a wise sailor to steer the ship of my life. The deep meaning of this proverb strikes a chord with me, and that's why I like it so much.

2. Carl, thanks for inviting me to view the big waves. However, I have no choice but to decline your invitation. It is too dangerous to go there right before a typhoon comes because the massive tidal waves may sweep us away. I don't think it's a good idea to risk our lives just for the excitement of viewing waves. Besides, if we should get trapped at the beach, search-and-rescue effort would be launched to save us, and that would increase huge social costs. Therefore, if you really want to, we can plan a safer wave viewing tour to China's Qiantang River. What do you think?

## 實戰演練

埃及古老的文字系統中「安卡」符號意謂「生命」。它包含一個長的垂直線與較短的水平線在頂端交會，與水平線交接的是一個底部尖起的圓形。

然而，安卡也是古埃及文化一個重要標誌，能以一個獨立物體存在。舉例來說，許多埃及神祇與法老的雕像皆手握安卡。十九與二十世紀挖掘皇室墓地時，考古學家發現上千個安卡。安卡常雕刻在墓穴門口。深入墓室會發現安卡出現在裝飾品與壁畫中。著名的雅赫摩斯‧納菲爾泰麗王后棺木上有其雕像：雙手胸前交叉，各握著安卡。安卡被認為能夠在通往來生的旅途上幫助死者，提供人間與永恆的連結。

安卡符號一經發現後學者便開始搜尋它的起源。1869 年，湯瑪士‧伊曼暗示道，正因它意謂「生命」，它代表兩性的生殖器官：線條代表男性、圓形表示女性。其他人認為這在胡謅，並提出各式理論。例如，其中一人認為安卡是女神伊西絲的皮帶鉤，另一人則認為是太陽從地平線上升。沒有人的說法獲得當代學者的普遍認可。

在現代，「新時代運動」採用安卡象徵力量與智慧，也同時是項鍊等珠寶的普遍設計。然而安卡真正的起源仍是個謎，埋藏於時間的迷霧中。

1. 答案為：⒟。此題判斷為 supporting details。本題測試第一段的細節內容，而且必須將本段描述 ankh 的細節文字，轉譯成圖像。掃讀後將第一段的關鍵字 "a long vertical line"、"a shorter horizontal line"、"cross the top end"、及 "circular shape" 圈出來，可知直線較長，而在頂端交叉的橫線較短，而且頂端上面是個圓圈，故唯有⒟選項符合這四項文字描述，故選之。

2. 答案為：⒜。此題判斷為 supporting details。掃讀後圈出⒜選項的關鍵字 "spiritual symbols" 及 "physical objects"，並在第二段第 2 行找到對應內容，可知 ankh 不僅是表示生命的精神象徵，也可作為裝飾的實體物質，故⒜為錯誤敘述。接著圈出選項⒝的關鍵字 "statues"、"wall paintings" 及 "coffins"，並在第二段第 2、6、7 行找到對應內容，可知這些地方都有 ankh 出現，故⒝正確。再來圈出選項⒞的關鍵字 "the dead"，並在第二段第 8 行找到對應內容，可知 ankh 可幫助亡者通向來世，故⒞正確。最後圈出選項⒟的 "the female's sexual organs"，並在第三段第 4 行找到

對應內容，可知 ankh 的圓形圈圈，象徵女性生殖器官，故⒟亦正確。

3. 答案為：⒞。此題判斷為 main idea。本題無法只靠找出主題句，來找出第三段的大意。所以可快速略讀本段內容，從第 2 行的 origins 和第 5 行的 various theories，可拼湊出本段的關鍵資訊可能為討論有關 ankh 起源的不同理論；再加上作者在本段也提出三個有關 ankh 起源的說法作為支持論點，故可確認⒞即為正答。

4. 答案為：⒜。此題判斷為 words in context。掃讀後，在第四段第 4 行找到對應的目標單字。接著利用上下文線索，掃讀圈出前一句的關鍵字 "remains a mystery" (作者用 mystery 暗示 ankh 的起源仍是個謎)，及後一句的關鍵字 "the mists of time" (作者用同義片語來「重述解釋」ankh 的起源因時間的迷霧而更難以了解)，可知 obscured 就是像謎一般，「讓人難以了解」，故選⒜。

## 回答問題

1. I will choose A—the ancient Egyptian ankh sign —as a lucky charm for my brother to give him a sense of inner peace and wish him good luck. Besides the meaning of "life," the ankh is also a symbol of power and wisdom, which I think are important for an examinee like my brother. With the ancient mysterious power, I am sure my brother will fulfill his true potential and pass the important exam with flying colors.

2. I don't believe in an afterlife beyond our present existence because for me, it is more important to live in the present. When we count on life after death, it is possible that we will idle away our time thinking there is always another life to make up for what we have missed and build our hope on an unrealistic castle in the air. Besides, the afterlife is the core concept of some religions, but there isn't any scientific evidence to convince me of its existence. I think it is just a comforting lie that people tell themselves to overcome their fear of death.

## 🕐 實戰演練

　　在日本，「御宅族」過去多指書呆子或土包子的冒犯字眼。今日，許多日本人已接受御宅族這個標籤，不再認為它是負面的字。御宅族用以形容尤其對日本動畫、漫畫、電玩有特定嗜好的狂熱愛好者。日本境外，御宅族不僅指對日本卡通與漫畫感興趣的人，也指著迷於一般日本文化的族群。

　　御宅族這個詞的使用始於 1980 年代，搭上當時流行的動漫。御宅族代表社會邊緣人的次文化，他們無法透過體育或學術上的成功來提升社會地位，改而專注於其他興趣。御宅族的概念是過著離群的生活、患有社交障礙的人，藉由觀賞動漫、閱讀漫畫來消磨時間。御宅族這個標籤在一位御宅族宮崎勤被發現殺害四名女童後，變得更加負面。事件發生後，宮崎勤被稱作「宅男殺人魔」。所幸，御宅族的壞名聲已不再，其定義也改成代表著迷某種動漫或電玩的人。現在有 42% 的日本人承認自己是御宅族中的一種。

　　御宅族通常專注愛好特定文化或種類如動畫、日本漫畫、電玩、角色扮演等的類型。動漫或漫畫分別是日本形式的動畫與漫畫媒體，且是大多數御宅族的主要興趣。

　　現今東京秋葉原地區是御宅文化的中心，含有許多展售動畫、漫畫產品的商店以及女僕與其他主題咖啡廳。女僕咖啡廳中，女服務生穿著與動漫相似的女僕裝。其他咖啡廳圍繞動漫或漫畫為主的主題，這些咖啡廳鼓勵顧客裝扮成自己喜愛的角色。

　　御宅族不僅需要克服形成他們今日生活方式的個人問題，更要克服一般大眾的恐慌與猜疑。儘管過去紛擾，御宅文化仍在日本與全球蓬勃發展。

1. 答案為：(C)。此題判斷為 supporting details。掃讀後圈出題目的關鍵字 "Japan's otaku culture"，然後在第一段可找到對應的內容，可知本題測驗第一～二段的細節內容。選項(C)的關鍵字 "increasing popularity of anime"，在第二段第 1～2 行找到對應內容，可知日本動畫流行助長御宅族興起，故(C)為正確答案。

2. 答案為：(C)。此題判斷為 main idea。略讀第二段首尾兩句後，即可發現第一句介紹 1980 年代御宅族的興起，而最後一句說明目前全日本有 42% 的人被界定為某種類型的御宅族，在略讀中間內容作資訊拼湊，即可確定本段內容是關於御宅族發展的歷史，故正確答案為(C)。

3. 答案為：(D)。此題判斷為 words in context。掃讀後，在第二段第 2 行可找到對應的目標單字。接著利用上下文線索，可在下面二行找到作者對 "outcasts" 所下的「定義」，可知 outcasts 即指社交技巧笨拙不安、無法藉由運動或學業方面的傲人表現來提升自己社會地位的「社會棄兒」，故選(D)最接近作者所下的定義。

4. 答案為：(D)。此題判斷為 supporting details。本題測驗第三～五段的細節內容。掃讀後選項(D)的關鍵字 "panic and suspicion"，在五段第 2 行找到對應內容，可知日本民眾對御宅族的害怕及猜疑並不會影響它在海外流行，故(D)為正確答案。

## ✎ 回答問題

1. Yes, I think I am heavily involved in Japan's anime fandom. I think the major appeal of anime lies in its great artwork and visual quality. In addition, the plots and characters in anime are also rich, interesting, and imaginative. For example, Hayao Miyazaki's *Spirited Away* is my favorite. The characters in it all have real personalities with both strengths and flaws, which make them more attractive and thus enhance their characters. They are just like real people, so I can easily identify with them and get some insights beneficial to my life. All in all, I think the anime fandom has helped reduce my academic pressure and added more color to my life.

2. Yes, I think I will give it a try because I have never been to such places and served by waitresses dressed in maid costumes. To me, having a meal in such a theme restaurant is like taking part in a costume party. If I am given a chance to go to the restaurant with the theme of *Spirited Away*, I will try to cosplay and dress up as "No-Face," a lonely and faceless spirit wearing a black robe without any facial expression. Chances are that I will encounter other characters in this film coming into life before my eyes. That will be very interesting!

## 實戰演練

　　當不同的光波長進入我們的眼睛時，我們看見不同的色彩。物體會反射並吸收特定波長而產生顏色。色彩理論試圖以合乎邏輯的方式組織色彩，並確定色彩如何互動、融合。源自於光源如電視等的色彩與源自塗料與染料的色彩遵循不同的規則。當混合不同色彩的光線時將產生白色；相反地，當混合許多顏料時將產生黑色。藝術家對色彩理論的了解很重要，因為他們只能使用有限的顏料創作一系列顏色。

　　色彩理論的歷史基礎是根據紅、黃、藍的色彩範本，這三色被認定是「原色」，其他色彩由原色產生。當混合兩個原色時將產生間色：綠色、橘色與紫色，例如，黃藍混合產生綠色。當混合原色與間色時將產生複色，複色名稱含兩個顏色，例如橘黃色。將這些顏色照邏輯排成一個圓，稱作色輪。艾薩克‧牛頓爵士在 17 世紀建立第一個色輪。今日我們知道能使用其他原色範本，例如印刷用的洋紅色、黃色與青綠色，螢幕用的紅、藍、綠色。

　　色彩調和是依據色輪，觀賞上賞心悅目的色彩組合，有許多色彩調和的組合，其中之一含兩個互補色 (色輪上相對位置的色彩)。當例如紅、綠的對比色放一起時產生明顯對比，而更突出。另一種色彩調和是由色輪上三個以上周遭色彩合成的圖畫。

　　要成為一位成功的畫家，如何創造你想要色彩的知識很重要，也有必要知道色彩如何和諧地相互作用，來創作一個令人印象深刻的作品，這也是色彩理論對任何藝術家或設計師而言重要的原因。

1. 答案為：(B)。此題判斷為 main idea。本題無法只靠找出主題句，來判斷全文大意，所以可快速略讀每段首尾兩句，拼湊資訊。略讀後，可知第一段介紹色彩的形成、第二段介紹色彩的基本原理、第三段介紹色彩調和原理、第四段強調色彩調和對於藝術專業人士的重要性，故選項(B)為正解。

2. 答案為：(C)。此題判斷為 supporting details。掃讀後(C)選項的 "circle" 及 "color wheel"，在第二段第 7 行可找到對應內容，可知將不同顏色作邏輯性安排，會形成色環，故(C)正確，為本題答案。

3. 答案為：(D)。此題判斷為 words in context。掃讀後，在第二段第 5 行可找到對應的目標單字 "tertiary color"。接著利用上下文線索，可在第 5 行找到作者對複色所下的「定義」：原色＋間色，即可形成複色，以及在第 6 行找到作者對複色的

「舉例」：它們的名稱會包含兩種顏色 (即一原色＋一間色)。選項(D)的敘述符合上面的「舉例」原則，故為正確。

4. 答案為：(A)。此題判斷為 supporting details。掃讀後圈出題目的關鍵字 "color harmony"，可在第三段找到對應內容。接著圈出(A)選項的關鍵字 "go well together" 及 "pleasing"，在 1～2 行可找到對應內容，可知色彩調和意指色環上不同顏色搭配時，可給人愉快的視覺感受，故(A)即為正解。

## 回答問題

1. My favorite color is blue because it is the color associated with the sky and the ocean, which always gives me a sense of peace and calm. In my view, the color blue not only is visually pleasant but also functions as a tranquilizer for me to get adapted to the fast-paced life. Besides, with a girl with fair skin, I think I look good in blue, and it really matches by skin. Whenever I wear blue dresses, I always receive compliments from others, which puts me in a happy mood. Based on the two reasons above, that's why I like the color blue so much.

2. I think a world without colors would be totally inconceivable! We would live our lives without the fun and variety from seeing colors, and that would be dull and boring or even chaotic. For example, we couldn't see colorful national flags, traffic lights, clothes, or even colorful flowers and plants in nature. Besides, we would lose the chance to describe people or things with colors, like "a man with green fingers," "a boy going purple with rage," "once in the blue moon," "golden opportunity," and so on. Therefore, we are blessed to live our lives with different colors, and we should treasure the fun and joy colors add to our world.

## 實戰演練

古希臘人將醫學設成一門獨立的科學。古希臘的醫生也考慮到醫學倫理，發展一套書面的行為準則。這成為眾所周知的希波克拉底誓詞，以希臘醫學創建人之一的希波克拉底命名。

誓詞要求醫生尊重病患的尊嚴，承諾絕不傷害病患和只推薦健康飲食。若要求安樂死，他們也必須拒絕用藥了結病患的生命。此外，他們發誓絕不開藥給「任何想摧毀胎兒的孕婦」。

黑暗時代 (Dark Ages) 過後，希臘醫學重新被發現並且對現代醫療科學的發展有所貢獻。16 世紀一些知名學校開始在畢業典禮上採用此誓詞，幾世紀以來它受封為醫師道德責任的指引。

然而，到了二十世紀，其中的細項對於特定複雜的議題，例如終止人類生命，似乎太過死板。今日，特定情形下終止妊娠是合法的，例如胎兒有先天性的缺陷。此外，「醫助自殺」的趨勢也開始浮現，例如當一位病人罹患絕症，承受巨大痛苦時。以上二例子皆允許醫療專業人員終止生命且被認為是個慈悲的選項。

最後，希波克拉底誓詞有了修正的版本。今日廣為使用的版本由 1964 年塔夫斯大學狄恩醫學院修正。它推崇尊重、同情病患的原意，但醫師現在也宣誓「奪去生命也是我的職權」。新版誓詞是全球許多大學醫學倫理課程的一部分，它反映了關於醫師責任的想法如何與時並進，但其所保留的部分展現了至今我們仍受古希臘的影響。

1. 答案為：(C)。此題判斷為 main idea。本文旨在介紹醫師誓詞的起源及發展，因此讀者略讀全文之後，可以了解醫師誓詞隨著時代變遷而有所修正，亦可在第五段第 6 行找到作者提示的重點 "doctors' duties have changed over time"，故選 (C)。

2. 答案為：(B)。此題判斷為 supporting details。本題測試有關古希臘醫師誓詞最初的細節內容。掃讀後選項(B)的 "diet"，在第 2 行可找到對應內容，可知醫生可給予病人有關健康飲食的建議，故(B)為正確答案。

3. 答案為：(D)。此題判斷為 supporting details。掃讀後(D)選項的 "compassion"，可在第五段第 3 行找到對應內容，可知原始的醫師誓詞即使經過修改，對病人的憐憫至今仍為醫生所應遵守的醫學

倫理，故(D)為錯誤敘述，為本題答案。

4. 答案為：(B)。此題判斷為 inference。利用掃讀找出 "**It may also be in my power to take a life**" 位於第五段第 4 行，利用資訊拼湊找到第五段第 1 行 "modified versions"，可推知這句話依據修正後的醫生誓詞內容，現代的誓詞內容便納入「醫生被允許必要時結束末期病人或天生殘疾胚胎的生命」，故(B)為正確答案。

## 回答問題

1. I am for "physician-assisted suicide" because I think dying a good death with dignity is more important than living a miserable and painful life. Everyone has the right to decide when his or her life should end and what kind of life he or she should live. Therefore, after careful consideration, if a terminal patient decides to end his/her life, we should respect his/her decision. On the other hand, sometimes the costs of treating a terminal disease is far more than one can afford and may become a heavy burden for the family. Besides, physician-assisted suicide has now been legal in countries like Swiss, Germany, Japan, Colombia, Albania and some states in the USA. Therefore, based on the two points mentioned above, I am in favor of physician-assisted suicide.

2. I think we should take the following measures to improve hospital security and provide medical staff with a safer working environment. First, we should pass laws or make violence prevention regulations to punish those who attack medical staff. In addition, hospitals should hire more security guards and cooperate with the police to curb such attacks. Doctors and nurses can also wear protective clothing to protect themselves from sudden violent attacks. I do believe that only when doctors and nurses are free from attacks will there be better quality of care and doctor-patient communication.

## 實戰演練

位於英格蘭中部的一個郡成為英國國內將「仇女」制定為仇恨犯罪的第一個郡。諾丁漢郡定義「仇女」這種仇恨犯罪是「因男性對女性的態度所引發針對女性的事件,包含單只因女性的性別而遭男性針對的行為」。這種仇恨犯罪包含言語或肢體傷害、街頭騷擾、性挑逗、不事先經過女性同意而用手機傳簡訊或拍照。

諾丁漢郡加入比利時與葡萄牙等其他歐洲國家的行列,將「仇女」,包含言語傷害等,制定為仇恨犯罪。一位比利時女製片人使用隱藏攝影機記錄在街上針對她的評論之後,該國通過這項法律。

英國境內女性組織的國際聯盟公布 2016 研究指出 85%、年齡介於 18–24 歲的英國女性曾「在公眾場合中受到不想要的性注目」,而且感覺有必要在晚上出門時訂定「安全計畫」保護自己。超過半數的受訪女性表示她們在公眾場合感覺不安全。

「終止暴力對待女性聯盟」的代理主席莎拉・格林評論:「我們進行這項調查是為了瞭解性騷擾的規模與其對女性生活方式的影響。如果女性須規劃她們的生活不受騷擾或攻擊,那麼她們並不自由。女性應該自由自在生活不受騷擾與暴力的威脅,無須計畫或限制自己的選擇以確保自身安全」。

諾丁漢郡的女性讚許這條法律,並將這條法律視為將所有仇女形式行為認定為仇恨犯罪的一部分,進而擴大仇恨犯罪定義的一大步,她們對新法律將讓諾丁漢郡變成一個更安全的居住地抱持希望。

1. 答案為:(B)。此題判斷為 main idea。略讀後找出文章第一句"A county in central England . . . by making it a hate crime" 即為主題句,後面段落列舉歐洲其他立法將「仇女」視為仇恨犯罪的國家,並介紹婦女組織所進行的相關研究及活動,對此法律作進一步的說明,故選項(B)為正確答案。

2. 答案為:(C)。此題判斷為 supporting details。掃讀後選項(C)的關鍵字"three European regions",在第二段第 1～2 行找到對應內容,可知目前只有三個歐洲地區將「仇女」列為仇恨犯罪,故(C)為正確答案。

3. 答案為:(D)。此題判斷為 inference。掃讀後將題目中"safety planning"圈出來,然後在文章第三段第 3 行找到對應的目標單字。接著利用上下文線索,在第四段找到作者關於婦女作安全規劃的

看法及解釋,可知如果一個地方夠安全,婦女出門在外,應該能夠像男性一樣可以自由安全地從事各種活動,也較不需要額外花費心神作安全規劃,故(D)選項即為 safety planning 所隱含的意思。

4. 答案為:(C)。此題判斷為 writer's tone。略讀後可發現作者以客觀的口吻和立場,引用名詞定義、統計數據及權威人士說法,來撰寫全文,當中並無個人情感或意見摻雜在內,故(C)為正確答案。

## 回答問題

1. Yes, I agree. Living a life free from fear is a fundamental right for all humans, including women. Therefore, they should live a life free from any forms of assault, harassment and discrimination. Besides, after the law is enacted, police action will also be involved to ensure women's safety and rights of living a carefree life. With the protection of the law, women will be able to stand up for their own rights and pluck up courage to report misogynistic incidents to the police. Therefore, I think we should make misogyny a hate crime to increase safety for women.

2. Yes, I think Taiwan is a safe place for women to live in. According to a survey conducted in 2014, Taiwan ranked world No. 2 in the world's top 10 safest countries. Compared with other countries, I think there is less misogyny against women in Taiwan, and cases of verbal and physical abuse or harassment on the street are seldom heard. So, by and large, women in Taiwan can live and work with a sense of safety and dignity. Besides, women may still need to do "safety planning" if they want to go out at night, but overall, they are safe in public places, even at midnight. In sum, Taiwan is a safe and friendly place with low rates of violent crime and robbery, and therefore it is a particularly safe place for women.

# Unit 13

## ⏱ 實戰演練

　　想像你在銀行排隊或搭乘地鐵上班，如果要你形容周遭的人，會認為他們在進行什麼活動？或許近來首先浮上心頭的是人們緊盯著智慧型手機。也許他們在玩遊戲、發簡訊、或只是瀏覽網頁。不管他們在做什麼，一定在消磨大多人認為是無聊的時光。

　　許多人承認用智慧型手機來擺脫我們生命中瑣碎、無聊時光是最容易的方法，然而，這可能不是一件好事。事實上，消除全部的「無聊」實際上不利於我們的生活。雖然我們可能不會覺得「無聊」有趣，但無聊時光實際上有益於我們的大腦。

　　「無聊」不該是一件需不計代價去避免的事，它反而是個贈禮。身處在受廣告、新聞與其他許多干擾轟炸的環境中，讓人驚訝的是許多人選擇持續看手機、使我們更加被手機分心。一些人認為大家不該這麼做，反而該欣然接受「無聊」，將之視作大腦能運用的空白時光。與其讓來自智慧型手機的刺激佔據大腦，不如讓心靈漫遊。這類的心靈漫遊使人們能拓展想像力，並再次文思泉湧。

　　有許多例子說明偉大的想法來自一段無聊的時間。我們常將這種時光稱作做白日夢。如果我們一直被手機佔據，沒有時間做白日夢了。難道我們宣稱失去一些東西是不公平的嗎？

　　下次你乘坐公車或排隊買票時，把智慧型手機放口袋吧，讓「無聊」稍微進駐，這可能會帶領你進入一個出乎意料的美妙境地。

1. 答案為：(D)。此題判斷為 main idea。本題無法只靠找出主題句，來判斷全文大意，所以可快速略讀每段首尾兩句，拼湊資訊。略讀後，可知第一段說明目前許多人滑手機消磨無聊時間的現象；第二段作者對此現象提出異議，認為這種現象對我們的生活有害；第三～五段作者進一步闡述他的看法，並提出空白的無聊有助發展創意及想像力，故選項(D)符合文章各段敘述大意，為正解。

2. 答案為：(C)。此題判斷為 words in context。掃讀後，在第二段第 3 行可找到對應的目標單字 "detrimental"。接著利用上下文線索，可在上一行找到作者用不同的話 "this may not be a good thing"，來「重述解釋」detrimental 的意思，故選項(C) harmful 的意思最接近 not good，為正確答案。

3. 答案為：(A)。此題判斷為 supporting details。掃

讀後圈出(A)選項的關鍵字 "technologies" 及 "distractions"，即為 1～3 段描述智慧型手機等科技設備，可讓人們隨時隨地更加分心，以排解無聊，故(A)為正確答案。

4. 答案為：(B)。此題判斷為 writer's attitude。略讀後可發現作者在第二段最後一行就指出無聊對我們的大腦有益。另外在三～五段，作者也繼續根據這個論點，並使用如 gift、embrace boredom、it might lead you to .... wonderful 等正面的敘述進一步闡述他的看法，可知作者對無聊的態度是「鼓勵的」，故(B)為正確答案。

## ✎ 回答問題

1. Kelly is a student who has to spend forty minutes taking bus to school every day, and the 40-minute ride is really a period of unbearable boredom for her. Last Friday, feeling bored on the bus, she took out her smartphone and started to phub it. She logged onto her Facebook, checked LINE messages and replied to them. After that, she decided to watch her favorite Korean drama on Youtube. She was so absorbed in it that she didn't noticed a pickpocket approached her stealthily, trying to steal her money. Fortunately, a passenger saw this and caught the thief on the spot. After the incident, Kelly has made up her mind to embrace the boredom of taking the bus instead of being a careless phubber.

2. I think it has changed our lives for the worse. First, we spend 3.7 hours a day on average staring at our smartphones, which has made our busy life even busier. Second, we may have poorer health and eyesight because of using the smartphone for a long time. Last, I think the advance of technology should connect people rather than make them feel more alienated. Now we talk to people more online than face to face, and this has also put the quality time for our family or friends at risk. Based on the above reasons, I think smartphones have brought our lives more disadvantages than advantages.

## 🕐 實戰演練

「universe」中的字首「uni」來自拉丁文「一」。直到近代，這個 1580 年代隨著現代科學崛起而發明的字似乎是一個合適的選擇。世人多認為單一的物質宇宙來自最初的宇宙大爆炸 (the Big Bang)。報告同時指出，宇宙是以光速擴展，所以儀器永遠偵測不到宇宙的邊界。雖然這引發驚嘆，但令人安慰的是：望遠鏡觀察到的宇宙有熟悉的四維，在時間與空間中運作。

然而，現行版本的宇宙理論完全弄錯了。1980 年代，天文學界的發現支持一個革命性新理論。這項新發現太驚人以致必須改變語言來描述之。也就是說，科學家必須移除「universe」中的「uni」。

當天文學家測量宇宙大爆炸期間創造的引力總量時，資料顯示一些驚人的結果。它指出該引力總量遠大於目前偵測到宇宙的現存量。所以這些額外的引力消失在何處？合邏輯的解釋是最初的大爆炸產生無數次爆炸，或許創造了無限個其他宇宙。另外，這可能也產生超出我們想像的不尋常特質。

因此，「multiverse（多重宇宙）」成為科學單字的一個特色。「multi」在拉丁文中意謂「許多」，也見於單字「multiple（複數）」，故似乎符合實際情形。這個新發現的複雜性顯示了人類知識的侷限。我們甚至無法觀察到自己宇宙的盡頭，所以更不可能探索這些遙遠的宇宙。我們只知道他們可能存在於遠方某處。然而，我們之中的許多人仍使用傳統的「universe」，或許因為這些宇宙外的宇宙遠超出能讓我們反覆思考的理解範圍。如同詩人 T.S. 艾略特寫道：「人類無法承受太多真相」。

1. 答案為：B。此題判斷為 supporting details。本題測試第一段的細節內容。掃讀後選項(B)在第 3～4 行找到對應內容，可知大爆炸為造成宇宙起源的原發性爆炸，故(B)為正確答案。

2. 答案為：D。此題判斷為 reference。掃讀後找出指涉題 It 位於第三段第 2 行，接著利用上下文線索，判斷 It 在此代替前面一個句子裡的 "something extraordinary"，而此「令人驚奇的事物」的內容，閱讀下面 3 行的詳細說明後，可知是指大爆炸所產生的額外引力的「驚人發現」，故選擇答案(D)。

3. 答案為：C。此題判斷為 supporting details。掃讀後將題目中的 "take the 'uni' away from the word 'universe'" 圈出來，然後在第二段最後 1 行找到對應的類似詞彙。然而將 uni 從 universe 中移除的原因，卻要略讀第三段、找出此段大意後，才知科學家此舉乃是要藉由改變文字，來支持革命性的理論：除了我們目前所在的宇宙外，還有其他無數平行的多重宇宙存在，故(C)為正確答案。

4. 答案為：A。此題判斷為 inference。文章針對宇宙觀點 "universe" 和 "multiverse" 討論，推論這類的內容最有可能在科學雜誌中出現，故選(A)。

## ✏️ 回答問題

1. Yes, I do. Since there is infinite multiverse, it is rational to assume that other intelligent life exists elsewhere in space. Some unsolved and incredible mysteries on Earth can serve as evidence to prove the existence of aliens, such as the Nazca Lines, Crop circles, or Stonehenge. As for what they look like, since they are more advanced creatures than us, I think they can change their appearance anytime at will. For example, they may disguise themselves as a purple-skinned creature with a huge square face. With three big oval eyes in red, green, and blue, they can see through everything. I think the strangest part is that it has neither a mouth nor a nose. How weird!

2. If I had a chance to go on a space trip for free, I would definitely take it because I have been interested in becoming a space tourist since I was little. With this opportunity, I could appreciate the beauty of outer space with my own eyes. I would also have the chance to acquire an insider's knowledge of space travel and skills to cope with emergencies in space. Best of all, I think going through zero-G training, experiencing weightlessness, as well as floating around in space must be very cool!

# Unit 15

## 實戰演練

　　地球的海洋日益受到污染，是眾所皆知的事實。海洋中的石油及其他化學物質正對依賴著海洋而生存的生物造成毀滅性的影響。然而，另一個少為人知的污染源是塑膠廢棄物。

　　最新研究指出，我們的海洋被大量塑膠廢棄物包圍。據估在太平洋兩處收圍積了 70 萬 5 千噸的垃圾；一處位在日本沿海，而另一處則在加州附近。它們一起被統稱為成為 「太平洋垃圾帶 (The Great Pacific Garbage Patch)」。那裡漂浮的垃圾大多是塑膠廢棄物，隨著時間過去會分解為較小的塑膠碎片或微粒，但絕不會消失。很不幸，海鳥通常將這些塑膠碎片或微粒誤認為食物吞下肚。

　　1960 年代開始，科學家已開始分析海鳥吃下的塑膠廢棄物數量。1960 年代僅有 5% 的海鳥胃中有塑膠，然而在 1980 年代則遽增至 80%，目前則高達 90%。這些數據對我們海洋的未來及居住的生物而言，並不是個好兆頭。海鳥胃裡所發現的大量塑膠廢棄物，應被視為警訊。但我們該如何處理海洋的塑膠廢棄物危機呢？

　　最近一項大有可為的點子是名為 「海洋垃圾桶 (the Seabin)」 的發明。此裝置能自動過濾海水，並移除石油、燃料、化學物質和漂浮垃圾如塑膠瓶等。這些海洋垃圾桶可以設置在港口、河川、湖泊等處。然而，重要的是我們必須謹記在心，單靠科技的力量並無法解決此嚴重的環境問題。世界各國政府必須攜手合作，對抗海洋塑膠廢棄物的問題。如果我們現在不採取行動，終有一天海鳥會變成人類腦海中一段模糊的記憶。

1. 答案為：(D)。此題判斷為 main idea。略讀後找出第一句 "It is a well-known fact that the planet's oceans are becoming increasingly polluted" 即為主題句，之後再略讀各段首尾兩句進一步確認，可知本文目的在於喚醒讀者對於海洋塑膠垃圾污染的關心，故選項(D)為正確答案。

2. 答案為：(B)。此題判斷為 supporting details。掃讀後圈出題目的關鍵字 "threat" 及 "marine animals"，可在第一段 2～3 行找到對應內容，可知選項(A)漏油、(C)塑膠垃圾及(D)化學廢棄物，皆威脅到海洋生物的生存；文章中並未提及選項(B)漂流木 (屬於天然垃圾，非人工廢棄物)，故為正解。

3. 答案為：(C)。此題判斷為 supporting details。掃讀後圈出 (C) 選項的 "seabird plastic consumption"、"eighteen times" 及 "1960s"，在第三段第 2～3 行可找到對應內容，可知現在 90% 的海鳥吞食塑膠，是 1960 年代 5% 的 18 倍，故(C)為正確答案。

4. 答案為：(B)。此題判斷為 words in context。掃讀後，在第三段第 4 行找到對應的目標片語。接著利用上下文線索，掃讀圈出前幾句的關鍵數據 5%、80%、90%，及下一句的作者用 "abundance" 和類似字義的 "warning"，暗示這些數據預告將來如果我們不積極解決此環境問題，海鳥未來將在有更多塑膠垃圾的環境中生活，然後吃進塑膠垃圾的比率還會再增加，故選項(B)為正確答案。

## 回答問題

1. First, we should stop using disposable plastics and replace them with reusable versions. Second, we should stop buying bottled water and bring our own reusable bottle instead. Third, we should not buy beauty products with tiny plastic microbeads because these microbeads do not break down easily. If we can start to change our living habits, we will make a big difference to our marine ecology.

2. As we can see from the picture, I guess the seabird must have lived in an area full of marine litter or plastic waste. When it went out searching for food, it must have mistaken plastic waste for food. After that, the seabird could not digest the plastic waste, so the waste got stuck in its stomach, leading to its weight loss and death in the end. Now, its body has decayed, but its feathers and bones as well as the plastic waste in its stomach haven't. So I can see its stomach full of plastic bottle tops, a plastic cigarette lighter, and other plastic debris. The scene is really scary! I think if we don't take action to reduce plastic input into the oceans and do better waste collection and recycling, more and more seabirds will fall victim to ocean plastic waste in the future.

| Unit 1 | Unit 2 | Unit 3 | Unit 4 | Unit 5 | Unit 6 | Unit 7 | Unit 8 | Unit 9 | Unit 10 | Unit 11 | Unit 12 | Unit 13 | Unit 14 | Unit 15 |

# *Unit 16*

## 🕐 實戰演練

達爾文獎是個半開玩笑的獎項，頒發給死於自身愚蠢的人。他們對人類的貢獻就是把自己從基因庫中移除。

達爾文獎的命名來自發表演化論天擇說的查爾斯‧達爾文。「天擇說」指存在不合適基因的生物在其能夠繁衍前去世，使物種得以隨著時間改變或演進。因此，達爾文獎定義不合適的基因是「愚蠢」。

達爾文獎始於網路剛興起時，最早提及達爾文獎的文章發表於 1985 年：描述該獎頒發給已逝世、「移除自己的基因於人類基因庫之外」的得主。獲獎者不只需死於自身愚蠢，也需死得有趣好笑。例如，一名恐怖份子 2000 年寄發郵包炸彈，因郵資不足退回寄件人。恐怖份子渾然不知寄件人是自己，拆信而死。

要成為達爾文得主，你必須喪失繁衍能力，因此你必須已死亡或不能生育。獲提名者必須是因為自己嚴重誤判而死亡或無法生育，他們須具備為自身決定負責的能力。也就是說，他們也必須是成人、沒有心理缺陷。最後，獲提名的故事來源必須有根據，例如來自報紙與電視報導。

著名的得獎包含詹姆士‧波恩，他試圖在友人駕駛卡車時維修車子，當他在卡車下方時，衣服鉤到某物，最後被發現「捲進傳動軸」。另一位得主在密西根州，他決定徒手移除落在車子的電纜，結果觸電死亡。一名男子試圖從 70 呎高的橋上以 70 呎的彈跳繩索一躍而下，卻忘記繩索會伸展。

如你所見，這些獎項的確悲劇，卻很難不嘲笑這些人荒謬的死法。

1. 答案為：ⓒ。此題判斷為 main idea。文章第一句即為主題句，略讀後發現此主題句即清楚點出具半開玩笑性質的達爾文獎之定位及頒發對象，故選項ⓒ：「達爾文獎：死亡從沒如此滑稽過」涵蓋文章主題，也說明它不是那麼嚴肅的獎項，為正確答案。

2. 答案為：ⓓ。此題判斷為 supporting details。掃讀後選項ⓓ的關鍵字 "exclusively" 及 "dead"，在第四段第 2 行找到對應內容，可知除了死亡之外，達爾文獎亦頒給無法繁衍、傳承愚蠢基因的人，故ⓓ錯誤，為本題答案。

3. 答案為：ⓒ。此題判斷為 supporting details。掃讀圈出題目的關鍵字 "requirements"，可知本題測試第四段符合達爾文獎五項條件的細節內容：

有趣、因「自己」糟透的判斷力而導致「自己」死亡或不孕、成人、無精神疾病、消息來源可靠。選項ⒶⒷⒹ符合這些標準，但選項ⓒ錯誤，因為得獎者愚蠢的死亡必須由自己造成，而不是他人，故選之。

4. 答案為：Ⓐ。此題判斷為 words in context。掃讀後，在第四段第 2 行可找到對應的目標單字。接著利用上下文線索，可在第 1 行找到作者用同義字 "be unable to reproduce" 來 「重述解釋」 sterile 的意思，故選項Ⓐ「不孕的」即為正確答案。

## ✏️ 回答問題

1. What I have learned from the Darwin Awards is that we can look at one thing from different or even opposite perspectives. For example, contrary to its corresponding Academy Awards, the Golden Raspberry Awards are awarded in recognition of the worst in films. Another example is that the parodies of the Nobel Prizes, the Ig Nobel Prizes, honoring achievements that first make people laugh and then make them think. Seeing these examples, maybe next time when life knocks me down, I will remember to look at them from another angle, taking them lightly or even laughing at them.

2. When I was a third grader, one day I found a chain letter in my drawer. The letter threatened me to make twenty copies of it by hand and then pass them on to my friends. If I broke the chain and refused to forward the letters to twenty people, I would have bad luck or even die a horrible death. Out of fear, I did it as instructed. Later, I found that it's only superstition and that nothing bad would happen to the chainbreaker. Knowing this, I felt relieved and realized how stupid I had been. Therefore, sending chain letters is the stupidest thing I have ever done in my life.

這是一套為愉閱英語而生，

一套能體驗英閱樂趣，

## 英文讀寫萬試通　精采內容

### 閱讀技巧篇：Unit 1-3

前3回為您說明閱讀技巧，讓您輕鬆閱讀英文、攻破閱讀測驗。同時貼心彙整近六年大考高頻率出現的大考閱測題型。緊接著提供二篇大考閱測文章與題目加以驗證解釋前述技巧，讓您完全理解閱讀方向和解題關鍵。

### 實戰演練篇：Unit 4-16

後13回文章主題豐富、包羅萬象，探討最熱門的議題；編排由淺入深，漸進式培養閱讀素養，提升閱讀實力。每回有1篇文章、4題仿大考的題目和2題開放式回答問題，訓練獨立思考與批判性思考能力。開放式回答問題為仿大考寫作練習，提供看圖、主題、簡函寫作等題型，抓住大考的脈動。

✔ 本書附解析本，完整提供文章翻譯、答題思路與答題範例。
✔ 學校團體訂購附3回贈卷。
**本書可搭配107課綱的加深加廣選修課程「英文閱讀與寫作」。**

一套能開拓視野見聞，

一套能厚植英語實力，

一套讓人愛不釋手的系列叢書。

三民網路書店
www.sanmin.com.tw

「英文讀寫萬試通」與
「解析本」不分售
80336G